Weight   For   It

by Kelly Morgan

WEIGHT FOR IT

<u>Foreword</u>

I killed and buried an old friend today. It was a swift death after a few well-positioned blows. Blunt force trauma, I believe it's called. It was a sobering service, with only me in attendance, and it took everything in me to pay my last respects. I had been so obsessed for so long; it started to control my every move. The entire relationship was a toxic rollercoaster, which took me over a year to dissolve. I had ended the relationship so many times before, only to beg for my friend to take me back after a few days.

If I doubted myself, my friend was there to show me the truth, no matter how brutal. I found myself not doing things because I knew my friend would disapprove. My friend was seldom forgiving and could make me feel so bad about myself. I did everything I could to gain my friend's approval, but in the end, I had to let go and say goodbye. But this time, goodbye meant forever—no more bullshit. I killed my friend and there is no coming back…ever!

Murder? No, it wasn't murder. It was more like self-defense. I decided to put myself first and defend the little bit of pride I had left. I had hit rock bottom and my friend was right there, letting me slowly descend into a haze of low self-esteem and self-loathing.

Now, you're probably thinking, how could I do this? How could I take a life; especially a friend's? Well, I was driven to this moment by a series of life-changing events. My friend was there the entire time—most of the time mocking me, very seldom cheering me on. Always incessantly mocking! I could have sworn I heard laughter a few times too.

I thought about all the events that had built up to this moment. I leaned my head back and closed my eyes. I think the turning point was about a year ago. I had hit my rock bottom, but somehow, found a way to sink even lower.

Chapter 1

It was a few years ago that I once again had to do something about my weight gain. I'm not even sure how it happened. I mean, I have always been a 'big girl'. My mom called it being *big-boned*. Society calls it fat.

It all started one fall. I was lying in bed thinking about waking up when a knock at the door jostled me to get out of bed. It was Boonie. Boonie had been my best friend since middle school. I nursed him through a bad marriage and practically everything else before and after that. He was gay and had married a woman he met in college—I know, a tragedy waiting to happen. He married her because she was pregnant.

I've known Boonie most of my life. I met him in the summer, just before we started fifth grade. His Auntie Gloria owned a new hair salon downtown, and I went one Saturday with my mom. I remember gathering my good barbie and coloring books and shoving everything into a bookbag. I wanted to take more barbies, but the rest had been chewed up by the family dog, Duke. My last surviving barbie, who I had affectionally named Foxy Brown (after the Pam Grier character in the movie) had also been chewed on, but not as badly as the others. Her face was a little deformed from a bite mark, and her blonde hair was choppy, matted, and uneven. My brother told me that I couldn't name my barbie Foxy Brown because she was white, but I didn't care. Anyone can be named Foxy Brown, I said back defiantly. And the name stuck. Soon everyone in the house called my barbie Foxy Brown.

I was playing with Foxy Brown in the salon waiting room, when I saw Boonie at the soda machine. Even then, he had style. He wore stonewashed jeans, a blue-collared shirt, a brown bomber jacket, and Adidas sneakers. He counted his money and put it in the machine. He caught me staring at him, and I quickly looked away. Once he had retrieved his soda, he walked over to me.

"Hi," he said.

"Hi," I responded.

"You wanna soda?" he asked, smiling at me.

"I don't have any money."

"I have money. I will buy it for you. I'm Boonie, my Auntie Gloria owns this salon. She does hair, and sometimes nails. She knows all about that stuff–fashion, makeup, shoes, clothes…" His voice trailed off.

"My mom is back there getting her hair done," I said, pointing to the back of the salon.

"Come on," He grabbed my hand and pulled me toward the soda machine, "What do you want?" he asked.

I looked at all the choices, "Red cream soda," I responded.

He put the money into the machine and pushed the button for the soda. He handed it to me, "Come on, we can go sit in the back room, I have a TV and Atari."

He motioned for me to follow. I ran back, grabbed my bookbag and followed him to the breakroom. We sat on the sofa, drinking our sodas. I fixed Foxy Brown so that she was sitting too. That is when he took an interest in her.

"What is wrong with your Malibu Barbie?" he said, laughing.

I looked at Foxy Brown. *She didn't look that bad*, I thought to myself.

"My dog chewed her up," I said.

"Oh. Well, what's wrong with her hair?"

"Her name is Foxy Brown," I said, sounding a little defensive.

He howled with laughter, "Foxy Brown? Like the movie?"

I didn't answer. He noticed that I wasn't laughing with him and smiled.

"I can fix her hair," he said.

"What?"

"I can fix her hair," he repeated. "I can cut it so that she looks a little better." He reached for Foxy, and I grabbed her and pulled away, a suspicious expression on my face. I had let another boy, my brother, touch my barbies and they always ended up with a pulled-out arm or leg.

"What do you know about cutting hair?" I asked.

"A lot. Hand me those scissors on the table."

I remember looking at the scissors and then looking at him. I think he could read my mind because he said, "I won't hurt her, I promise. I will cut her hair and she will look really good. We can even dye it so she won't be blonde."

Something told me to trust him, so I handed him the scissors and Foxy Brown. He took off his jacket and went to work. I was surprised when he successfully cut her hair into a really cute bob. We bonded over Foxy Brown. He told me everything he knew about hair, makeup, and fashion, which was more than anyone I knew. It was that afternoon that we became best friends. I spent the summer with Boonie at his Auntie's salon, and from then on, we told each other everything. I told him I was always getting teased for being heavy, and he told me that he had always felt different. He didn't like sports, although his parents pushed him to do "boy" things, and he wanted to spend all his time at the salon.

By the time we reached high school, Boonie and I were inseparable. We were always together. I loved being around him because he had so much confidence and was always so sure of himself—the exact opposite of me. He didn't care what people thought. The only opinion that mattered to Boonie was that of his mother's, and he went to great extremes to keep his sexuality a secret from her.

****

I remember when he told me he was getting married. I can remember it like it was yesterday, even though it was years ago. We had met for coffee and a catch-up date.

"So, guess who's getting married?" he said, sipping his chai tea.

"Who?" I said, mixing the sixth sugar into my coffee.

"Me," he responded casually.

I instantly stopped stirring my coffee.

"You can close your mouth," he said while smiling.

"Boonie, what do you mean- getting married?!"

"Well, you know I've been experimenting right? I mean, I know I'm gay and all, but to please my mom, and supposedly Jesus, I started dating girls. So, enter Trina. I met her in my econ class. She's really cool. We went out a few times. She has the most fabulous wardrobe—the dresses, the shoes, the makeup. Oh! My! God! It was everything! I had to hold myself back from raiding her closet."

He continued to gush over Trina's closet until I finally had to stop him.

"What the fuck, Boonie? What are you talking about getting married? Does she know that you're gay? What the fuck is happening? You haven't even had sex before and now you're telling me that you are getting married?" I paused long enough to catch my breath until a realization hit me, "Wait, have you had sex with her?" I asked, staring at him. "And before you respond, if the answer is yes, and I'm just finding out about it, I'm hurt. Secondly, I didn't even know you were dating. Still hurt."

He looked at me with those soft brown eyes and took my hand. His smile slowly turned to a kind of frown. Not a sad, *sad* frown, but a serious, *I fucked up* frown.

"She is pregnant," he said.

I could barely compose myself.

"What the fuck!" I said, standing up. But when I saw the embarrassed look on Boonie's face, I slowly sat back down.

"You need better training," he grumbled, sipping his tea. "Look," he started intently—"I know I fucked up. I didn't even enjoy it, but I cannot tell my mother that I am gay. I would put her in an early grave. I know this is a big decision, but I think I will make an excellent dad. Don't you think?"

"But Boonie," I said—"Does she know you are gay?"

"Oh, girl, no. But I'm going to do the honorable thing and marry her," he said, without an ounce of excitement in his tone.

"Boonie, why?" I asked, "Just tell her. I will be there for you if you want."

"Too late girl, both our mamas know, and they've set the date. I didn't think shotgun weddings were real, but here I am. I really wanted to pick you to be my best man, but I have to settle for my cousin, Patrick."

I watched him sip his tea. I felt so sorry for him.

"You wanna split a fudge brownie?" I asked. He looked at me and nodded his head yes. We ate four between us that afternoon.

They did get married and had a little girl named Ivy. The marriage was doomed from the start—mostly because Boonie swore off vagina. After a year and some months, the marriage ended badly. It's bad enough your man leaves you for another woman, but when it's another man… Trina lost it. She went after Boonie with everything she had. In the end she got everything, and he got visitation rights. It wasn't until Ivy was in her teens that Trina finally let it go and Ivy and Boonie could develop a good relationship.

Boonie is a really good dad. How many girls' dads know about makeup, fashion and hair? To this day, Ivy and Boonie are inseparable.

****

Boonie continued to pound on the door, and when that wasn't enough, he started on the doorbell.

"I'm coming!" I yelled.

"Girl get yo' ass up!" I could hear him shout back.

I slowly rolled out of bed—I mean *roll* in the literal sense. I wrapped my tattered robe around me, and slowly walked to the front door. I unlocked it, turned around, and started for the kitchen without pausing.

Boonie opened the door and stepped into the house. He was always so fashionable. He wore a pair of tight grey, pleated slacks with a collared pink shirt and grey tie. He was carrying his statement pink and grey man purse, which I have been trying to steal for months.

"Girl, what is going on here?" he said, looking around my cluttered house. "What you been doing or… not doing?" He picked up a dirty bowl, a cup, a half-eaten bag of chips and two soda cans from the coffee table.

I looked at him and said, "I don't want to go." Our eyes met for just a moment before he walked into the kitchen. "I'm not listening to this because we already had this conversation. You promised you would go. It's my weekend without Ivy, and honey, I need a drink. So girl, we are outta here!" he said.

I could hear him turn on the water at the kitchen sink. I stood in the living room trying to find a reason not to go. I did promise, but I was in no mood. I mustered up the courage and walked into the kitchen.

"Look, I know you want to go, and I know that I promised, but I don't feel well. Boonie, I'm tired." I tried to present my best 'I'm really sick' facial expression.

He didn't even look at me, "You're going. Now, what's going on with your hair, girlfriend? Please go and take a shower. Have you been in bed all day?"

He stood with his back to me, washing dishes. I wanted to scream or cry—I couldn't decide which.

"Look Boonie, I really don't feel good," I groaned.

"Nope, not happening. I'm going to finish up here while you go take a shower. Then, we will find you something fabulous to wear, and I will do your hair and makeup, okay?" He finally turned around and looked at me. His eyes were soft, and his smile was warm. How could I say no?

"Okay, okay. I'm going to shower. Thanks for cleaning up."

"Girl, we need to re-evaluate your life," he commented, turning around towards the sink. "I don't know what is going on with you, but a night of fun can't hurt."

"It can't help," I whispered as I left the kitchen.

Boonie was excited about our 25th high school reunion, which I had no desire to attend. I didn't really like the people back then, so why should 25 years make a difference? I definitely wasn't popular in high school, and spent most of my time doing school work or hanging out with Boonie.

High school is not kind to fat girls—at least not to me, anyway. I was constantly being teased because of my weight. Boonie was naturally tall and thin, and in contrast, I was short and round. We got the nickname '10' when we were together. The teasing never seemed to bother Boonie, but to me it felt like absolute torture.

Boonie knocked on the bedroom door, "Are you ready to get fabulous?" he asked.

"I guess," I said as I opened the door. Immediately, a look of disgust contorted his face.

"Sweatpants?" he asked.

"I'm just wearing this until I— or rather you, decide what I should wear." I sat on the edge of the bed and watched him walk over to my closet.

He put his hand to his chin, as if deep in thought and started rummaging through the clothes.

"Hmm," he said, "Not this, or this, definitely not this…" His voice trailed off.

I lay back on the bed and closed my eyes. I secretly hoped he wouldn't find anything to his liking.

"Ah, I think I have found it. Yes, I have always loved this dress on you. This is it!" He emerged from the closet with a black cocktail dress that I had purchased for my son's college graduation a few years ago. It was cute, but I only wore it once. I was confident it wasn't going to fit.

"Okay, get dressed. Let's see it on you," he said, excitedly.

I stared at the dress. "I don't think it will fit. I bought it a few years ago. I can just wear that flower dress I always wear to work. I know that fits."

Boonie frowned. "Look, I know you don't want to go and you're only doing this for me. I really appreciate it, and wouldn't want to go with anyone else. I think you would look fantastic in this dress."

"What size is it, Boonie?" I asked in a hushed voice.

He searched for a tag, and then replied, "The tag says… 24."

"It definitely won't fit. I bought that dress a few years ago. I am now a size 28," I could only admit that to Boonie because I knew he wouldn't judge me.

He put the dress back in the closet and sat next to me on the bed.

"Okay, so you've gained a few pounds, it's no big deal," he said.

"A few pounds? Did you not hear me? I'm a fucking size 28, Boonie. I weigh almost 275 pounds! I'm tired all the time. I have no energy. I'm depressed. My life is a complete joke. My husband left me because of my weight gain. My kids drop subtle hints about working out, or joining a gym, or some new diet. Don't they think I see? I know exactly what I look like. I literally eat all day Boonie because I'm so fucking depressed and I can't do anything else. Eat and cry. That's what my life has become…" I buried my head in my hands and let the tears flow down my cheeks.

Boonie didn't say a word. He stroked my back and sat there with me. Finally, after several moments he said, "So, what are you going to do about it?"

"Huh?" I asked, wiping my tears.

"What are you going to do about it?" he repeated. "You have control of your life. If you don't like something, change it," he said. "Look, I know you have struggled with your weight, but you can turn this around, if you believe you can."

I wiped my tears. "I'm so tired and miserable. I'm tired of being fat. I think I have hit rock bottom… and my heaviest weight ever."

We sat in silence for a few more moments until Boonie spoke, "You know, since you've hit bottom, the only place to go is up! So, why don't we make you over? A whole new you! New you, new life?!"

I looked at him with tears still running down my face. I tried to smile. Boonie was always there for me and he was here now. He really was a good friend.

"It sounds like work," I said dryly.

"Oh, it's work honey, but it will be worth it. Trust, Boonie. I know," he said, smiling. "Now, get your ass up and put on that flower thing you call a dress and let me work my magic with your hair and makeup."

"Remember when kids would call us 10?" I asked.

"We are a 10 because we are fabulous. Fuck those hoes! Now get dressed. I'm going to find us some music and go grab my hair and makeup bag from the car. When I get back, I want you dressed," he said, and left me to search for the dress I usually wear.

This was the worst part of my day—getting dressed. He made it sound so simple, but getting dressed was gut-wrenching every time. First was the underwear—*extra-extra-extra-extra*-large panties, which by the way, are hard to find. Then, the bra. I can never find a bra that fits. My latest size is a 44DD. It seems to fit okay but leaves deep marks into my sides and shoulders. Not to mention, the side fat that hangs over.

I struggle, twist and turn and manage to get the bra on. I sit down on the edge of the bed, breathing heavily. Putting on a bra has become a sport. I can't believe I'm out of breath. I thought about wearing a body shaper, but honestly, what's the point? I probably couldn't get in it anyway.

Now, for the dress. It really wasn't as much of a dress as it was a muumuu. I found it at a thrift store, and it doesn't look too bad with accessories. Besides, I had given up being fashionable a long time ago. I really hate putting on clothes, period. I have reached the point in my life where I am uncomfortable in my own skin. I don't need anyone else to loathe me—I have heaps of that for everyone. I looked in the mirror and I didn't like what I saw.

I took a deep breath and flung the dress over my head. So far so good, until I get to the zip-up part. I don't know why I buy anything with zippers. After a bit of a struggle, I zip up the dress, but all I can think of is a circus tent and I'm the elephant in the flower dress, or maybe the fat lady—I can't decide.

I could have sworn I heard circus music…

Chapter 2

The Rosemont Class's 25th reunion was held at an upscale hotel downtown. The ballroom was decorated with class memorabilia, balloons and streamers. There was a slide show playing on the main wall, continuously flipping through pictures of days long past. It was horrible.

I've never seen Boonie so excited. He loved this shit. He could have fun wherever he went, it didn't matter to him.

We stopped at the main table to check-in and pick up our name tags. I could feel all the insecurity I felt when I was in high school flooding back to me. Did I mention that high school is not kind to fat girls?

Boonie walked up to the table and announced himself, "Boonie Alexander is here, so let the party begin," He looked at me, winked, and smiled.

The lady at the table looked up, "Boonie, is that you? You look great. Oh, my God! It's been so long. How are you?"

Boonie stared at her as if to say *ahhh excuse me bitch, who are you?*

She must have gotten the message and happily announced herself. "It's me, Carrie Parker! I was on the Glee Team and Spirit Squad. I remember you. You used to hang out with that girl… I don't remember her name… she was kinda frumpy… heavy set. I remember we used to call y'all 10… you were the one and she was the zero, for obvious reasons," she laughed.

Did she not see me standing next to Boonie, or she just didn't care?

Boonie shot me a quick look and took my hand, "Oh, I remember you—a Spirit Squad hoe. Y'all really thought you were doing something, with your jumps and kicks and lame-ass cheers. I heard you gave 'spirit' to the entire football team, honey—passed around like a football. Such a shame that you didn't age well, honey," Boonie shook his head, "It's just too bad, the last 25 years don't seem like they were kind to you. Oh well, see you inside, Carrie Parker."

Boonie pulled me with him, and he started for the ballroom door. I looked back at Carrie Parker. Her mouth was still open as she watched us walk away.

We found an empty table and sat down. We didn't speak for a few moments, until I broke the silence, "Thanks," I said.

He looked at me, "Oh honey, you never have to thank me when I get the opportunity to put a bitch in her place. It felt good. Besides, we don't give a fuck what these hoes think. We were fabulous then and we're even more fabulous now."

"So, remind me why we came here again?" I asked. "Come on Boonie, why the fuck are we here? I know you haven't missed these assholes. You're up to something. I know you. Spill it."

"Okay, okay. I heard that Jackson might be here."

"Jackson? Oh, my God! You brought me here to be your wingman?"

"Now, calm the fuck down. I need you. You're my girl, and I need you with me so I can see him again."

"How did I know there was going to be some drama tonight," I said, throwing up my hands and rolling my eyes, "Here you go with this shit. Jackson? After all these years, Boonie? That doesn't even sound like you. There's more, Boonie. What are you not telling me? Wait, Jackson wasn't gay in high school, was he?"

"Girl, I always knew he was gay. I follow him on Insta and he came out five years ago. Can you imagine all those years in the fucking closet? Anyway, I guess all the gay pride stuff gave him the courage to admit it."

"What do you mean you follow him on Insta? Wait, how long has this been going on? You've never mentioned this before."

"One day, he hit me up on Insta and we started following each other. That led to DMs, and then phone calls, facetimes… He doesn't live here, but when the reunion was announced, we decided to meet here."

"Wow. I'm shocked. A little hurt, but happy for you. I can't believe you didn't say anything to me."

"You've been going through your own shit; I didn't want to add my drama. You know how I get."

We both smiled. It was going to be a long night.

****

I didn't think the night would ever end, or Jackson would show. After several glasses of 'punch' and barely any food, I was feeling a little tipsy. Just like in high school, Boonie was more popular than I was; I watched him work the room from my seat. He talked and laughed with various people and found it necessary to bring everyone he encountered to the table where I was sitting. I think he was trying to make me feel included.

"Just bri…ng me more of this… de…liciousssss punch. Stop… bringing people… just punch…" I said, slightly slurring my words.

I'm not sure how long I sat at the table drinking, but I had the sudden urge to pee. I slowly stood up and staggered into the women's bathroom. I found it empty and decided to use the stall at the very end. I went inside and closed the door. I was getting ready to sit down when I heard the main door open.

"Oh, my God! This has been so much fun. I really miss seeing my old team!"

It was Carrie Parker and some of the members of the old spirit team. I listened as they continued to talk.

"I know. It has been too long," a woman said.

"It's been so nice to see everyone. Time hasn't been good to all of us. Did you see Grant Walker? He looks so old," Carrie said.

"I know and what about Lee Moore? Didn't you date him, Sandy?" one of the other women asked.

"A million years ago. He did not look good."

They all laughed in unison.

"Did you see 10? They are still a 10, scratch that—more like 100 now!" Carrie laughed.

"10?" one of the other women said.

"Oh, you remember, Bryan— well Boonie, and that heavy frumpy girl he was always with. When they stood next to another, they made a 10, remember? They actually came together and are still a 10. I mean, if I were that fat, I would put a bullet in my head," Carrie said, in between bouts of laughter.

"Oh yeah, I remember her. I've seen Boonie walking around but I haven't noticed her," one of the women said.

"You can't miss her; she's wearing a large flower muumuu. I bet she hasn't stopped eating in all these years!"

They all howled with laughter and left the bathroom.

I suddenly felt sick and vomited on the floor. I could feel tears run down my cheeks. I wanted to leave. I managed to get out of the bathroom but didn't go back into the ballroom. Instead, I headed for the lobby and out the front doors.

I started walking, and then realized, I wasn't anywhere remotely close to my house. I pulled out my phone and requested an Uber.

20 minutes later, I was in the back of a Hyundai Sonata with Randy as my driver. He is nice enough, but a little chatty for me.

I leaned my head back and let out a soft groan.

"Rough night?" Randy asked.

"The roughest," I replied. My stomach did flip flops as my head ached. Note to self—no more reunion punch.

"I'm glad I picked you up. Things have been slow tonight, at least until the bars close. I like driving Uber because it gives me time to practice my acting skills— I'm an actor, by day. I have been auditioning for parts during the day and driving at night. It really seems to work, and I can use different costumes when I drive," Randy said.

"Do you have on a costume now?" I asked.

"No. I only wear the costumes when I am auditioning for a character piece. My latest audition is for an infomercial for men's hair loss. I'm trying out for the *after* guy."

"The after guy?"

"Yeah. You know, at first you see a man; sad and depressed with no hair. Then, you try the product and then, they show me— the *after* guy. I'm what it looks like when you use the product."

I tilted my head slightly forward so I could see Randy's hair. It was thick and black.

"You'd make a great after guy," I said, leaning back against the chair.

"I know, right. I even have a few lines. Want to hear them?"

"Sure, go for it," I groaned.

He cleared his throat and spoke, "I used to wear hats all the time to hide my baldness. Now, with Hair Hooray, hats are a thing of the past"—he paused for a moment—"Well? What do you think?"

"Hair Hooray?"

"That's the name of the product. How did I sound? Convincing?"

"Yeah, I'm convinced. If I were a bald guy, I would get some."

"There is more, but I can't show you while I'm driving. I'm supposed to throw off my hat, shake my head from side to side and run my fingers through my hair. And of course, smile."

"Wow! Well, I hope you get the part, Randy."

We pulled up in front of my house and I let myself out of the car. "Good luck," I said, starting for the front door. I was glad the night was over. Once inside, I went directly to bed, but couldn't sleep. My head was pounding from the reunion punch.

I thought about the incident in the bathroom. I thought about Randy and his potential acting role as the *after* guy. I was always the *before*, never the *after*. A flood of emotions hit me like a wave—more like a tsunami. High school was not kind to me, but after I graduated, I decided to make some changes. I thought if I made some grand gesture, I could wipe away the past, not look back and focus on the future. That was the only time I was the *after* person.

I committed to losing weight and I did. I joined one of those pre-made meal programs and followed it religiously, but it was expensive. However, finding the cash to pay for it wasn't that difficult because I was still living at home and going to school. I had to check in every week, weigh in and pick up my food for the following week. I did this for about eight months, lost sixty pounds and looked great. I went from 250 to 190 pounds. I told myself I was finally the *after* person.

All the weight loss went directly to my head. I started feeling better about myself and started dating and sleeping around. I *never* dated in high school. I never had a boyfriend. I was a virgin until I was 20. Not only had I dropped the weight, but my common sense also went right along with it as well. I just knew if a guy wanted to sleep with me, it was that he really liked me. I was pretty and desirable. It wouldn't be until much later in life that I understood that that statement isn't true. However, at that moment, sex equated to love and thin equated to being beautiful.

I dreamed of getting married and having the perfect relationship. I slept with every guy I dated during those times. It would make me feel cheap after the moment, but just the fact that someone wanted to be with me was enough to make me forget how it made me feel after.

I dated whoever asked me out. It didn't matter. I was just so happy to get the attention from the opposite sex. I was on a high—none of the guys ever stuck around very long though. I was good enough to sleep with and that was about it. I was really starting to feel worse about myself, when I started dating Matt. Matt was in my psychology class and was the finest guy I had ever seen. He had straight pearly white teeth, light brown skin, an afro and the softest brown eyes in the world. I fell in love the first time I saw him. When he asked me out, my head damn near exploded. I immediately said yes.

We dated for about two months before reality brought me back down to earth. I had weighed less than I had ever had in my life and felt great. Funny thing, when I left the program, I was afraid to eat. I had built up a strange fear that I would immediately gain the weight back once I started eating.

One night, Matt and I were lying in bed watching TV. I had started sleeping over about four weeks ago, and it was great. I would imagine that we were married and the most popular couple in our group. It was a Friday and we had decided to stay in. I loved being in a couple. It was nice to have someone to do things with. I found myself saying things like, 'my boyfriend and me', or 'my boyfriend does this or that'. I think it drove Boonie crazy, because we didn't see one another when I was with Matt. Bonnie used to call them, "The Matt Months".

Anyway, we were in bed when I had a craving for popcorn. I actually wanted a hot fudge sundae, but I had read popcorn wasn't fattening. When it came to Matt and food, I was never true to myself. I wondered how I could sustain a relationship where I didn't eat and when I did, I would make sure I was alone.

I left the bedroom and returned with a big bowl of popcorn. I jumped into bed and began popping kernels into my mouth.

Matt looked at me with a look of disgust and said, "That's fat girl shit!"

I immediately stopped eating. The words hung in the air—*fat girl shit.*

I looked at him and managed to say, "What does that mean?"

He wore a somber look on his face and replied, "Fat girls eat in bed, thin girls do not. Eating in bed is fat girl shit!" he said so matter-of-factly, and with almost no emotion. As if this was a well-known fact in the thin girl community.

My feelings were hurt. It was as if he unmasked the fat girl hiding underneath my thin body. I can't say skinny because I also learned that 195 pounds for me wasn't skinny. Matt also helped me with that little *tidbit* of information.

"Do you think I'm fat?" I asked, not wanting to hear his answer. I honestly thought he would have at least said no, but the hits just kept on coming.

"You are not skinny, if that is what you are asking. I rarely date big girls, but you have such a great smile. So, I decided to try it."

I was speechless, wounded, mad, hurt, sad and embarrassed all in one instant. He noticed the look on my face and continued to speak.

"Don't get your feelings hurt. There is no shame in being heavy. I mean if you weighed more, we probably wouldn't be dating, but I like that you are thick in all the right places," He smiled and leaned toward me, but I pulled back. Was I supposed to be in the mood? Did he just call me heavy? I thought heavy was the former me, the 250 pounds me, not the newly-transformed-195-pounds me.

"So, I'm some charity case that you decided to try? 'Let me get in my community service hours and date a fat girl?'"

"What are you getting so upset about? You should be happy to be my girlfriend. I'm a great catch," he said, leaning back into his spot.

"So, if I weighed more than I do now, you wouldn't date me? It wouldn't matter if I have a great personality, funny, caring, smart, beautiful? That wouldn't matter? How I look is the only thing that matters?"

"You would think you'd be happy because I'm being honest. Would you date me if I was a big fat guy?"

"I date you because I like you. I like spending time with you. How you look is secondary," I said, trying to sound morally right.

"So, how I look had nothing to do with the reason you said yes to me when I asked you out?" he asked.

I didn't answer because I knew he was right. I did date him because he was so incredibly good looking. He wasn't very smart, and he was definitely shallow and loved to talk about himself, but I was happy because I was dating someone I thought the fat me could never date. I didn't like where the conversation was going, so I didn't answer.

I felt horrible inside. I could feel the self-loathing bubbling up inside me. I replayed back the things Matt had just said to me. I was still the fat girl in his eyes, and mine too. We broke up a few weeks after that. Things were never the same. He made me feel worse about myself when I was with him than when I was alone. It didn't do me any good to lose all the weight if I didn't feel good about myself.

****

The memories of the phrase *fat girl shit,* swirled in my head. I was lying in bed thinking about the past and realized things haven't changed all that much. Here I was, even heavier than I was then. *At least then, I was dating,* I thought to myself.

I closed my eyes and let the reunion punch settle in my stomach. I slowly drifted off to sleep, while thinking *fat girl shit* thoughts.

Chapter 3

I opened my eyes and instantly felt the headache flood my temples. I groaned and rolled over and with one eye, peeked at the clock. It was 8:30am. I lay there thinking about the events that transpired last night. I wondered what had happened with Boonie and Jackson.

I was thinking about calling him when I caught the scent of brewing coffee. I stayed put and drew a few more breaths, just to make sure I was really smelling coffee. Then, I heard singing coming from the kitchen. I slowly sat up and got out of bed. I grabbed my tattered robe and decided to investigate.

When I reached the kitchen, I found my daughter, Sabrina, singing and dancing. She had on headphones and did not hear me come in. I watched her as she sang and danced. She was beautiful. She wore her hair short and natural. She had on a pair of jeans and t-shirt. Sabrina had been blessed with her father's genes. She got his long torso and slender build. I blessed her with an ass, round hips, and thick lips.

As she danced, she turned around and saw me standing, watching her. She smiled and took off the headphones.

"Morning, Mom," she smiled, "You don't look so good."

"I was out with Boonie," I said while hugging and kissing her.

"That explains everything," she laughed, "Coffee?"

I nodded my head and sat at the kitchen table. I watched as Sabrina poured the coffee. She had always been a happy, level-headed girl. She placed the coffee pot back in its place and sat down.

"What's on your agenda today, Mom?" she asked cheerfully.

"Nothing. Maybe cleaning the house. Why?"

"No reason. I really just came by to see how you were."

"I'm fine Bri, you don't have to check on me. I'm a big girl."

"Well, ever since you and Dad broke up, you don't seem to leave the house much."

"I leave the house," I protested, "I was out just last night with Boonie"

"Boonie doesn't count mom," she said matter-of-factly.

We sat in silence while drinking our coffee. If I know my daughter, and I do, she can't stay quiet for too long.

"Hey mom. I was thinking… a new gym opened up not far from here, would you wanna join with me?"

"What kind of gym?" I asked, thinking about what Boonie had said about taking control of my life.

Sabrina seemed to be excited that I didn't turn her down immediately. This wasn't the first time she had asked me to join a gym and I had said no to her earlier requests.

"It's a boxing gym. They teach like kickboxing, Muay Thai, tai chi… stuff like that. We could get our Bruce Lee on. I thought it might be fun."

I sat for a moment and thought about what Boonie had said; *new you, new life*. So, I responded, "Okay, I'll join you."

Sabrina damn near fell out of her chair and choked on her coffee, "Really?"

"Sure, why not? I've decided that I have to do something about this weight, and exercising can't hurt."

Sabrina looked at me and smiled. "Okay then, we can go over there tomorrow… no, make that Monday… and sign up. This is gonna be fun, Mom! I'm proud of you," Sabrina reached over and hugged me. I had a feeling Boonie had put her up to this, but I hugged her back anyway.

****

After hours of house cleaning, I decided to get online and research weight loss. I hadn't really ever taken my dieting seriously. I opened a web browser and typed in the words "weight loss". My search yielded millions of results. Weight loss is a 72-billion-dollar industry. Countless diets promising weight loss in a few days and pills that would work without *work* or the frustration of dieting. Every day there was a new program claiming you could be 'ten pounds thinner in five days', or the exercise program that promised fast results if you could only get your fat ass off the couch.

I was overwhelmed with all of the information. All the programs promised results and success, but first we need your credit card. Nothing is free. Some of the ads were so compelling and played on my emotions, that I almost purchased SkinnyYou - the latest wonder drug that could have me thin and trim in 30 days, no dieting or exercise. I just needed to part with six payments of $75 per month.

After several hours of searching, I decided the first thing I would do is purchase a new scale. My current scale was old and no matter who stepped on it, it always read 180 pounds. I figured this was a good place to start. I thought about ordering one online, but quickly changed my mind. I mean really these days, you don't have to leave the house for anything, but I thought an outing may do me some good. I had been a recluse for the past couple of months, so some fresh air wouldn't hurt. Besides, my hangover was gone, so why not? I grabbed my car keys and headed out the door.

I decided that I would spare no expense on the new scale, so I went to *Scales and More*. The scale section was ridiculous. Who knew there were so many different kinds of scales? I always thought scales were simple things, you step on them, they in turn reflect your weight. I had no idea how difficult my choice would be. Because I wasn't sure what to buy, I started out with price. I had decided that I didn't need the most expensive scale, but I also didn't think buying the cheapest one was a good idea. I was astonished to see a scale priced at $279. I quickly decided that was too much and went lower. The price war I was having inside my head was starting to give me a headache.

I was about to give up when I heard a voice.

"Me. I'm what you are looking for."

Expecting to see a salesclerk, I turned around. But no one was there. I was alone.

"I must be hearing things," I said out loud. "Definitely no more reunion punch."

"You heard me. Pick me. Down here on the bottom shelf, way in the back."

I looked around, but I was alone, "Hello?" I called.

"Down here, bottom shelf in the back."

I bent down and looked at the scales on the bottom row.

"You're getting warmer, sister," the voice said.

I moved the scales out of the way until I saw a single scale way in the back. It wasn't in a box like the rest of them. I grabbed it and stood up.

"You got it sister. I'm the scale you need," the voice, said again.

The voice startled me and I dropped the scale. It made a loud bang as it hit the floor.

"Watch it sister! I'm not fancy like those new models."

I stood there with my mouth open. Was this scale really talking to me? Was I having a stroke?

"Can I help you?" a voice startled me from behind. I jumped and turned around to see its possessor. I was relieved to see it was a salesclerk, "Ah, no I was just looking for a scale and dropped this one," I said, pointing to the scale on the floor in front of me.

The salesclerk smiled and picked up the scale.

"This model has been discontinued. I'm surprised it is even on the shelf. Do you need help picking out a scale? There are so many choices," the salesclerk said.

I wasn't sure what was happening. I managed to get some composure back, "Did you hear that?" I asked the salesclerk.

"Hear what?"

"You didn't hear another person speaking?" I asked.

The salesclerk looked around, and then, back at me, "No, I'm sorry. Are you feeling okay?"

I stood there staring at the salesclerk. I started feeling hot and sweaty. My mouth was dry, and I could feel my heart racing.

"I'm fine," I managed to say.

"Okay, did you want to look at some other models?" the clerk asked.

"No. I've changed my mind," I said. I turned around and left the store.

By the time I reached the car, I was in a full-blown panic. I couldn't decide if I was: A. losing my mind; B. Having a stroke or a heart attack; or C both. I fumbled for the car keys and managed to unlock the door. I jumped into the car and closed the door. I closed my eyes and started breathing heavily. *Inhale through the nose* I told myself, *out through the mouth*. I did this several times until I started feeling a little better. *I'll feel better once I eat*, I told myself.

After several minutes, I started the car and headed for *Burger, Burger, Burger*.

I had been eating out a lot lately. Cooking for one can be depressing.

I pulled into the drive-thru and ordered my usual, double bacon cheeseburger, large curly fries, large root beer, and chocolate shake. I come here so much that the *Burger, Burger, Burger* employees and I are on a first name basis. I pulled up the window and was greeted by Tyrone.

"Hey, there she is!" he said gleefully.

"Hi, Tyrone." I handed him my debit card. After he swiped it, he handed it back and said, "It will just be a moment," before walking away from the serving window.

Tyrone reappeared with my bag o' food, and I happily took it from his hands.

I put the car into drive and slowly drove away from the drive-up window. I pulled into a parking spot and parked. I opened the bag of food and began to eat. "I am losing my mind," I said out loud.

****

Monday mornings are always the worst for me, and today was no exception. I didn't sleep well because of my almost nervous breakdown, and I had a doctor's appointment at 9:00 a.m. I grabbed my robe and made my way to the kitchen to make coffee.

On the kitchen table was a large bag and a note. I picked up the note and read:

Mom – you are going to need these for class. Be ready on Monday at 7pm. Love S.

I looked in the bag and pulled out two black boxing gloves, a pair of workout pants and a workout shirt.

"She is serious," I said out loud and put everything back in the bag before making coffee.

There's something about going to the doctor that is unsettling to me. I think it's because I know they will mention my weight and tell me how unhealthy I am. Then, I will get a lecture on my BMI and how I'm obese. The sound of the word *obese* makes me feel 50 pounds heavier. To make matters even worse, I looked up the word obese and it means grossly fat or overweight. Grossly!

I sat in the waiting room, patiently waiting for my name to be called. Finally, after 20 minutes, it was my turn to go behind the door. A small petite girl in pink scrubs greeted me.

"Hi, I'm Leoni. Can we get your weight?"

I nodded, wishing I could say 'no'.

I followed her to a large medical scale. I took off my shoes, jacket and purse and stepped on the scale. I watched as she moved the weights all the way to the left where the zero was, and the balance bar was floating in the middle. She moved the bottom weight from zero to 250. Then, she moved the top weight until the balance bar floated in the middle of the balance window. She quickly wrote down my weight and smiled.

"Okay, let's go into exam room four and I can get your blood pressure."

I picked up my belongings and followed her into the exam room. I watched as she picked up a blood pressure cuff. She softly grunted as she tried to wrap it around my arm, but it became quickly obvious that it was not going to fit.

She smiled at me and said, "I'll be right back, I need to find a bigger cuff."

She was gone for about two minutes and returned with a very large blood pressure cuff. This cuff fit much better, but I couldn't help but notice the words 'Extra-Large Adult Cuff'. She quickly took my blood pressure and wrote it down.

"The doctor will be in to see you shortly," she said and left the room.

It seemed like an eternity before the doctor entered the room. She was a short blonde woman who wore too much makeup and perfume.

She came into the room and introduced herself.

"Hi, I'm Dr. Walker. What brings you in today?"

"I have been having some breathing issues and just wanted to make sure everything was okay," I said.

She looked at my chart and sat down on the little stool in front of me.

"Well, let's take a look," she smiled. "Can I listen to your heart and lungs?"

I nodded and watched as she placed the stethoscope up to my chest.

"Take a few deep breaths for me."

I followed her instructions, not once taking my eyes off of her face. She listened intently and then sat back.

"The first thing we need to do is lose some weight. Your BMI number is very high. Obesity can cause all kinds of problems such as hypertension, diabetes, stroke, coronary heart disease, the list goes on."

"So, I'm obese?" I said, sounding defensive.

"You are overweight, and it is probably the cause of most of your health issues," she answered sternly. "I'm going to give you a 1,500 calorie a day diet to follow. You may want to try to take daily walks and become more active. There is no magic pill I can give you. You have to be willing to do the work to lose the weight."

"Well, I'm going to start taking a boxing class with my daughter," I said.

"That is a start, but don't overdo it. It takes time to lose weight. I would recommend you get a good scale too," she said, smiling. "I will be right back with the diet information."

She left the room. I sat there in silence. I could feel myself wanting to cry, but I held back the tears. The doctor returned with the diet and handed it to me.

"I want to see you back in three months," she said. "You can schedule the appointment with the front desk on your way out."

I wanted to ask her questions about diet pills, and a weight loss surgery that I had read about on the internet. I wanted to tell her that I thought a bathroom scale had spoken to me, but her tone was quite dismissive. I probably would have never mentioned the scale, but I did have questions about losing weight the right way. She just handed me a diet. I didn't need to see a doctor to get a diet. There are literally hundreds of diets available on the internet. She didn't even address the reason I came in for a visit. It was by far the worst doctor visit I had ever had. She basically called me obese, gave me a diet plan and sent me on my way. I could feel the tears running down my face as I walked to my car.

Chapter 4

After visiting the doctor, I decided that I needed to take matters into my own hands. I found myself back again in the *Scales and More* parking lot. It had taken me two days to return, but here I was. I had spent the last two days eating my emotions and feeling sorry for myself.

I told Sabrina I would go to the gym with her, and I thought it was a good reason to buy a scale. I would start dieting and exercising at the same time. The weight will fall off, and then, everything will be better. I had convinced myself that being thin, or at least thinner than I was, would fix all my issues. Once I was no longer obese life would be better for sure.

I walked into the store and went directly to where I was before. I began hunting for the perfect scale. There were so many choices. I picked up the electric scale that measured BMI. I started to turn and head for the checkout counter when I heard the voice again.

"That's not the scale for you. Look again," the voice said.

I turned around, but there was no one in the aisle but me. I looked at the scale in my hand and put it down. As I set it down, I noticed the same scale I saw last time—not in a box, just sitting on the shelf. *Didn't the clerk say it was a discontinued model?* I thought to myself. I picked it up—no bells or whistles. It didn't monitor BMI or have fancy display monitors. It wasn't digital, and it seemed older and bulkier in contrast to the other scales.

I picked it up. It was heavier than the first scale. It was white, and instead, of a digital output it had a dial and arrow—definitely an older model. I examined it from all sides looking for a price tag but couldn't find one. I noticed a salesclerk passing by and decided to ask them for assistance.

"Excuse me. How much is this scale?"

The salesclerk smiled and walked over to me. I handed her the scale and she examined it. She had a puzzled look on her face.

"I really don't know. I didn't think we had scales like this on the shelves." She handed it back to me.

She looked around to see if anyone else was around. When she didn't see anyone else but us she said, "Look, I don't think we even sell this model anymore. I can let you have it."

"How much?" I asked.

"You can have it," she said. "No charge."

"Really?" I said, smiling. It must have been my lucky day. I thought someone was looking out for me. She nodded in response, "Are you sure?" I asked, not wanting her to get into any trouble.

"Sure. Let me grab you a bag and you can take it," She quickly reappeared with a large shopping bag, and put the scale inside.

"I am doing inventory tonight and I know that we discontinued this model a while ago. I don't want to count any more than I have to," she said, while handing me the bag. "Consider it a gift."

I took the bag from her and smiled. *This was a sign,* I told myself. I left the store feeling pretty good about my luck.

The drive home was as per usual—no strange voices lurking about. I had convinced myself it was all in my head. When I arrived at my house, Sabrina was there in her workout gear.

"I'm so excited you are coming, Mom. It's going to be a blast," she said, trying on a pair of boxing gloves.

"I'm not sure if I'm going to like it, but I have decided to make some changes in my life. I bought a scale and I'm going to start my diet tomorrow," I exclaimed triumphantly.

Sabrina frowned, "What diet?"

"Why do you have that look on your face?" I asked. "I have a diet plan the doctor gave me."

"Doctor? What doctor?"

"I went to the doctor today, and she may have mentioned that I need to lose some weight," I said as I walked quickly into my bedroom to end the conversation.

Okay, I have tried many, *many* diets in the past and could not stick to any of them, but this time would be different; or so I told myself.

I placed my new scale in the bathroom. I decided not to step on it until tomorrow. I quickly changed my clothes and went back into the living room.

"Okay, I'm ready."

"Good. Did you get the gloves?" Sabrina asked.

"Yes. They are still in the kitchen."

Sabrina grabbed the gloves and handed them to me.

"Let's go!" she said. And just like that, we were headed to the boxing gym.

****

We pulled into the parking lot of an old warehouse. I could feel my stomach turning and churning. I was nervous, but before I could say anything to Sabrina, she was out of the car and walking toward the front door. She shot me a glance that definitely said *get out of the car, Mom*. So, before I changed my mind, I picked up my gloves and slowly got out of the car. Sabrina waited as I took my time walking to meet her at the door.

We entered and the smell of sweat mixed with what I thought as Bengay hit us in the face. I suppressed an urge to cringe and followed Sabrina as we walked through another doorway into a large open space. In the middle of this room was a boxing ring. There were people in all areas of the space. Some punching heavy bags, others were doing crunches or sit-ups, and some were in the ring boxing. I felt my stomach drop. There was no way I could do any of these things. I started to call out for Sabrina, but a voice from behind startled me.

"Hi, are you here for the Beginner's Muay Thai Boxing class?"

I turned around to see a tall, good-looking (who am I kidding, fine ass) Mexican man. He must have been at least six feet tall. He had long black hair and a slight mustache. I couldn't help but stare at his several, and I mean *several*, tattoos. Sabrina answered him.

"Yes, I'm Sabrina. I spoke with Felix on the phone when I signed up."

"I'm Felix. Nice to meet you, Sabrina and friend," he said looking at both of us. "I'm glad you came. I will be teaching this class. The first thing we need to do is wrap your hands. I can show you how. Follow me."

I watched him as he walked away.

"Muay Thai boxing class?" I said looking at Sabrina.

"Well, we're here now, so come on," she said, while refusing to meet my eyes.

I followed her to the area where the heavy punching bags were. Felix was standing there holding two rolls of cloth. He handed one of the rolls to me.

"So, before we actually hit anything, we wrap our hands for added stability." He talked through the entire process. Before I knew it, both my hands were wrapped, my boxing gloves were on and I had followed Felix to a section of the gym where five other people were waiting. Class was in session.

Only fifteen minutes had gone by, but I was winded and sweating. Felix had shown us how to throw an uppercut and hook. I thought my lungs were going to pop out of my chest. He gave us a two-minute break. Next, he demonstrated how to throw a jab and cross punch. We did this for another fifteen minutes. I started getting a cramp in my side. I wanted to stop.

I looked at the other people in the class. They all seemed to be doing better than me. No one was sweating as much as I was or seemed as winded. I started to feel embarrassed. Felix must have noticed my look of defeat, because he took an interest in my progress.

"Okay, I want you to take your time," he said. He held up both his hands, "Right now, let's work on form," he said while smiling. He told me to stand in a fighting stance and use his hand as a target to throw a jab. We did this several times. "Breathe," he would say. I didn't realize I was holding my breath.

For the next thirty minutes, we practiced the punches we had learned. By the time class was over, I was soaking wet. Felix walked around the space giving everyone a high five. I could barely extend my arm upwards.

"We have class again on Wednesday," he said. "See you then?"

I wanted to give him arousing "hell no" but his voice, though domineering was soothing to the ears. Not that he would ever be interested in me, but it had been a long time since a man was kind to me and showed any interest—even if it was his job.

I looked at Sabrina and nodded my head. I was still too winded to respond. He smiled and said, "Alright! That's what I like to hear."

By the time I got home, I was exhausted. I decided to take a hot bath and go to bed. I thought about getting on my new scale, but I had read that it was better to weigh yourself in the morning. Besides, I thought, maybe the scale would show that all that punching had paid off.

I woke up early the next morning. My body was sore, muscles I didn't even know I had, ached. My arms, shoulders, back and legs hurt. I slowly rolled over and stretched; it was that moment that I felt the muscle in my left leg tighten. The tightening turned into a full-blown charley horse. I managed to somehow stand and began to slowly limp around the bedroom. The pain was unbearable, and it felt as if it would last forever. As I continued to force myself to walk, the cramp gradually faded away.

I slowly made my way to the bathroom. I sat on the edge of the tub and rubbed my leg. *Hell*, I thought to myself, *even my wrists hurt*. I noticed the scale sitting on the floor where I had left it. I slowly stood up and walked over to it. Now, I don't know about you, but scales have been unkind to me my entire life. I was actually afraid of the scale—afraid of numbers and where the measuring line would stop. I took a deep breath and stood on the scale. That is when I heard the voice.

"Are you expecting a miracle?" the voice said.

I looked down at the numbers. I stepped off and then stepped back on, ignoring the voice.

"Seriously? How many times are you going to step on me? Nothing has changed in the past thirty seconds," the voice taunted.

"Shut up!" I said, stepping off the scale. "Fuck, all that work. My body is sore and I have nothing to show for it," I said out loud.

"It's only day one. Stick with it. Maybe next time I'll be kinder. You need to stop eating so damn much. Maybe try some fruit this morning or a boiled egg."

"Yeah, some fruit," I echoed back.

"You want the numbers to change, then you have to do something different."

I stepped off the scale and sat back on the edge of the tub. I felt defeated.

"Not only am I obese, I'm having a conversation with a scale. I'm seriously fucking losing it."

I decided the only thing to do was to shower, get dressed, grab some fruit and head to work.

****

My entire day consisted of me avoiding food. When I arrived at the office, there were some bagels for breakfast in the conference room—the good ones, with the brown sugar and walnut cream cheese. I grabbed an apple and left the conference room. I locked myself in my office all morning. Around noon, my colleagues were about to head out for lunch. I heard a faint knock at my door.

"Come in," I reluctantly said.

A very small petite white woman named Ellie peeked around the door.

"Hey, we're all going to that new burger spot around the corner. Do you want to come with us?"

"Thanks, but no. I have some work to get done."

Yes, I lied. What I really wanted to say was, *"Bitch, do I look like I need a cheeseburger?"*

"Can we bring you something back?"

"No, I will just go downstairs and get some salad from the deli."

"A salad? Are you sure? I'm happy to bring you back something?"

I quickly shook my head no, "I'm good. Thank you."

Ellie smiled and left my office. I really wanted that cheeseburger with fries. I could hear the group leaving the office. Once I knew they had left. I went downstairs to the small deli. I never ate here. They only sold fat-free salads and sandwiches. They didn't even have fryers, which is probably the main reason I never ate here.

The walk was painful, and I felt sorer than I did when I woke up. I decided to take the stairs, which was something I never did. But I was doing things differently, so I had to try and change my usual routine. Besides, I was only on the fifth floor, how bad could it be? It was slow going, but I made it. I gave myself a mental high five and slowly made my way into the deli.

I ordered a chef salad with light dressing and water. I found an empty table and sat down. It was better than eating in my office. I watched the people coming in and leaving while I ate my salad. I didn't even realize I had eaten every bite. I purchased two apples and oranges and went back to my office.

I started walking towards the elevator, but remembered I was taking the steps. *Whose stupid idea was this?* I thought. I walked to the steps and opened the door. Five flights. *Five flights going up.* My mind reeled, but I took a deep breath and started the long walk up to the fifth floor.

Winded and tired, I finally made it. I was horribly out of shape but gave myself a mental high five anyway. Tomorrow I would be better prepared and bring lunch and snacks, and maybe just maybe, tackle those steps again.

****

I sat in my office for the rest of the afternoon thinking about food. I thought about how much food was a part of my life. Food had been there to comfort me before, during and after my divorce. I thought getting married would solve all my problems. Again, I found myself in a war with my thoughts. If I lost weight and was skinny, someone would marry me. Fat ladies do not get married. Have you ever seen a fat lady modeling a wedding dress in magazines—*Bridal Bizarre* or *Your Big Day?* The answer is a big resounding, no.

I met my husband during what I call one of my eating phases. This is where I tend to eat everything in sight. I cannot help myself. I was tired of dating just to have sex, so I turned my sights on ice cream, burgers, fries, pizza, tacos, and other delicious foods. I was slowly gaining back the weight too. I had gained about fifteen pounds, which put me at 205 pounds—not too much weight, but enough for me to notice.

I was in the grocery store getting my weekly supply of ice cream and other junk food when Carl bumped into my cart. I hadn't even noticed him, because I was busy searching the ice cream cooler for Moosetracks, which are by far the best flavor of ice cream known to man.

"I'm so sorry," he said, sounding very sincere. "I didn't see you."

I looked up and saw Carl for the first time. He stood about five foot eleven inches tall, brown eyes, athletic build, clean shaven and had the most beautiful smile playing on his lips.

"Oh, it's okay. I shouldn't be blocking the aisle," I said, moving my cart out of his way.

He noticed the container of Moosetracks in my hand.

"Is that the last Moosetracks? It's my favorite," he said.

"Yes," I said. I'm not sure what came over me, but I handed him the container of ice cream. He smiled and took it from my hands.

"Can I interest you in a cone?" he smiled.

In the grocery store's parking lot, we had ice cream cones. He purchased a box of waffle cones and a large spoon inside the store. It was the sweetest thing anyone had done for me. We talked for another thirty minutes or so and made plans to meet up the next night.

Our romance was a whirlwind. I kept pinching myself to make sure I wasn't dreaming. I had finally found a man who would potentially marry me. I thought I had won the jackpot.

In the beginning, our relationship was good. He told me all things men are supposed to tell the woman they love—you are beautiful; I love you; you complete me. Okay, so maybe he never said the last one, but he did tell me he loved me and that I was beautiful. I believed him and fell under his spell. I loved him.

I like to believe we got married because of all that love, but truth be told, I think he married me because I was pregnant. I didn't know until I was well into my first trimester. I had started gaining weight like crazy, and I could not stop eating. It was so strange.

It was this time that I started to hear little comments like: Are you putting on weight? Should you be eating that? Didn't you just have one? These were harmless questions at the time, but what I didn't know is that these questions would turn into accusations.

When I discovered I was pregnant, I was hesitant to tell Carl. We had been together for almost a year, but the passion we had in the beginning slowly started to fade. I told him one Saturday afternoon while I was making brownies.

"Brownies, again? How many brownies can you eat?' he said, watching me fill the pan with the brownie batter. "You know you are starting to get a little chubby. You might want to throttle back a little," he said. It sounded harmless enough, but there was a sting in the way he said it.

I put down the brownie batter and turned towards him.

"I'm eating brownies because I'm pregnant. I'm gaining weight because I'm pregnant, so throttling back, as you put it, isn't going to happen."

He stood there gazing at me. I wasn't sure if he was going to faint, throw up or bolt for the door. We were both young, in our twenties—what did we know about raising a family?

Part of me became scared because it took him so long to say anything. I thought I might throw up. Finally, he spoke. "Pregnant? A baby?" he said, sounding as if this was the moment he learned how babies were created. "I'm going to be a daddy?"

I nodded my head yes. I smiled at him. I wanted him to take me in his arms and tell me that he loved me, but he didn't. Instead, he sat down and buried his face in his hands.

I didn't say a word. Finally, after several moments he spoke.

"Do you want to get married?" he said, quietly.

"Do you?" I asked.

"I guess. I mean, I love you, so why not? It would be the right thing to do," he said in a matter-of-factly sort of way.

I had gotten my secret wish; I was getting married. All of my problems would be solved. Oh, how so very wrong I was.

Carl and I stayed together, got married and had two more children after Zaire, my daughter Sabrina and the baby, Marcel. Motherhood was not easy. It is probably one of the most thankless jobs one can take, but I did it like a champ. I dedicated my life to my children. I would come home from working a ten-hour day, make dinner, and then check homework. I was the one to attend parent-teacher conferences, make sure everyone made it to their doctor appointments, as well as sports practices and games. I felt like a single parent.

Over the next 20 years, my weight fluctuated. Carl and I drifted apart after Zaire was born. We were already having issues, but I gained over 60 pounds with Zaire, and lost very little of it after he was born.

The comments had now turned to insults. To Carl, I had become an overweight monstrosity that only cared about food and nothing else. *Maybe he was right,* I had thought to myself.

My kids took all of my time and energy. I poured everything into them. I stop caring about myself. I think I may have had postpartum depression but was never formally diagnosed.

I remember the last argument Carl and I ever had. It was horrible. I was extremely heavy, depressed and lonely. I didn't really see Boonie that much, and the kids were off in the world, coming into their own. Being with your mom wasn't cool anymore.

I was in the kitchen, eating and reading, as per usual for me, when Carl came home from work. He had been promoted to Controller at his firm, and he was working more hours. We didn't really see each other at all. We stopped sleeping in the same bedroom months ago. He told me that he couldn't stand the sight of me anymore. I probably weighed around 240 pounds, give or take a pound.

"Funny to find you in the kitchen," he said and sneered at the same time.

I didn't speak, but just kept eating and reading.

"No dinner left for me or did you eat it all?" he asked, sarcastically. His words were harsh and cruel. I didn't look up; I just kept my eyes glued to the magazine I had in my hand. I wasn't reading, but I didn't want to look up.

"You know what?" he started—"All you do is eat. I'm so disgusted I can barely stand to look at you. You are a fat pig. If it weren't for the kids, I would be long gone. I should have never married you anyway. You were fat back then, and fatter now. I'm done. I'm leaving. I refuse to stay married to someone who is an embarrassment! You don't even care anymore, do you? No one, and I mean, no one wants to be married to a fat ass like you!"

I looked up, doing everything I could to push back the tears that pricked my eyes. His words only confirmed what I thought about myself. *I was a fat pig! I was worthless!* I wanted to yell back, shout, scream and tell him to fuck off; but at that time, he was right.

"Do what you want," were the only words I could muster.

Things were pretty dark for a while after the divorce. Luckily, I had Boonie, who managed to pull me somewhat out of the darkness. I was still heavy, but at least I was still standing.

****

By the time I got home, I had decided to wait to weigh myself. I felt like I had really done something great today. I ate a controlled amount of food and took the stairs for lunch. That should count for something, right? I found myself in the bathroom staring at the scale. I thought about my day and how well I had done. I wish someone would have explained weight loss and how the scale works, but I ended up finding out the hard way.

I walked out of the bathroom, and then instantly, turned around and walked back in, then out again. This was the beginning of many battles I would have with the scale. I walked back in and took off my shoes and clothes. I needed to make myself as light as possible. I stood in the middle of my bathroom—butt ass naked about to step on the scale. I had no idea that this would be a life-changing moment for me.

I slowly put one foot on the scale. My heart was beating rapidly. I wanted so much for the number to be lower. I put my other foot on the scale. I closed my eyes and held my breath, as if doing this would somehow make a difference. I slowly looked down at the numbers. The scale registered 274 pounds. I could feel tears swelling up in my eyes, and that is when I heard the voice. It was different from the voice I normally hear in my head, which is my voice.

"Really, tears?" the voice said. *"If you want me to change, I need you to focus. One day isn't going to get it done, now is it?"*

"What?" I said, wiping my tears.

"You hear me. You know exactly who I am," the voice spoke again.

"What?" I asked again, unsure as to whether I was hearing things correctly.

"Look, every time you step on me, I tell a story. I am how you are going to measure your life. I am going to be everything to you. I will always show you the truth. The name of the game is to lose weight, right? You want to feel good about yourself, feel worthy?"

I nodded in response.

"Okay then. If you want to be worthy of anything good in this life, then your focus is me."

I stepped off the scale. I know it sounds strange, but this scale talking to me seemed normal. It was at that moment I decided my weight loss journey would take on a new life. I didn't know I would become fanatical or even unhealthy in my choices. All I knew is that I wanted to feel good about myself. I wanted to feel worthy of whatever I desired. *I was missing something in my life and the scale was going to help me find it.* Or so I thought.

Now, I know a little something about weight loss, all the tips and tricks. I have been a life-long member of the Trying to Lose Weight Club. I have seen those *before* and *after* pictures, you know the ones where Carol lost 100 pounds using *blah blah* method. You see a picture of fat Carol, sad and unhappy, and then they flash to a picture of skinny Carol, who is, you guessed it, happy and smiling. Carol has found a new life once she lost that 100 pounds. I was always the fat Carol and I never, in all my years, transformed into the skinny Carol. I was forever the *before* photo.

Just as my pity party was beginning, the phone rang. It was Boonie. He always did have great timing.

"Girl, where have you been? I haven't heard from you since the reunion. What happened?" he said.

"Really? I thought you would have called me by now. But when I left, you were knee-deep in love with Jackson."

"Jackson is old news. It is true that you can never go back home again," he sighed.

"What happened?" I said, sitting up. Boonie was always good for a distraction.

"What didn't happen? He is just so boring—nothing like his IG. I'm now starting to believe you when you say that social media is a farce. His dick pics weren't even real. What is the world coming to when you can't even get real dick pics? So, before you go there, yes, we slept together, if that's what you want to call it. Don't ask for details, I'm trying to erase those ten minutes from my life."

"Ten minutes? I'm sorry Boonie," I said, trying to stifle a laugh. I did warn him.

"That makes two of us. Wait, you sound extra sad? What's going on?"

I told him everything; the doctor's appointment, the kickboxing class and hiding out in my office. I didn't mention that I was having conversations with my scale—so, almost everything.

"It's only day one girl, and it sounds like you did good. You need to celebrate the little wins," he said.

"Do you want to go to class with me tomorrow?"

"Hell no! That's all you. I will be cheering you on from my sofa. Besides, I got a parent-teacher thing for Ivy."

We talked for a while longer. Boonie could always make me feel better. He was not the type to wallow in pity parties for too long. He was always a good source of advice too. He told me to pack a lunch and eat breakfast before I go to work, and to take lots of snacks like fruit and veggies. I knew he was right, but to be completely honest, it sounded like work. Why is gaining weight so easy? I mean you can eat whatever, sit on the couch and voila! Weight gained. But to take it off, you have to exercise and eat right, drink water *blah blah blah*.

I took Boonie's advice and meal prepped for the next day, even planning out my breakfast. I knew it would be a struggle since I love night-time snacking, but it was even worse because I was starving after my day of restraint.

At night, when I am alone, is when I usually curl up with my remote, a selection of snacks, and eat away my feelings. For the first time in years, I went to bed hungry. Tonight was hard. And I didn't sleep well at all.

Chapter 5

When I opened my eyes the next day, I told myself that today would be better. I had packed a lunch, prepped my breakfast, and had a bag of healthy snacks to take to work. I thought it was funny how my entire day revolved around food. Nevertheless, I told myself it was going to be a good day. I marked the day in my head—day two.

I crawled out of bed. My legs and arms were sore. I did my morning routine with one slight change, I ate breakfast. I usually only have my coffee with a lot of cream and sugar, but today, I decided to go for green tea, water, a couple of boiled eggs and an apple. I carefully packed my lunch, which consisted of a tuna sandwich with spinach, a couple of oranges, two boiled eggs and a green salad. It seemed like a lot of food to me, but I followed my doctor's diet almost to the tee.

I spent my entire morning thinking about food. I never realized how much food consumed my thoughts. I thought about lunch and eating the sandwich and salad. I thought about the boiled eggs and oranges. I couldn't get food out of my head. I kept checking the clock. Why was the morning dragging?

By noon, I was like a crazy person. I made a mad dash for the kitchen and grabbed my packed lunch. I went directly to my office and closed the door. It took no longer than ten minutes for me to consume the entire sandwich, an orange and both boiled eggs. It was the best lunch that I had ever had. I was just about to start on my second orange when there was a knock at my door.

"Come in," I said, quickly wiping my mouth. It was Mr. Henry, who was hands-down the kindest boss I had ever had. He listened to me and let me make important decisions when it came to company business. We had absolutely nothing in common, but food. His wife was constantly making pies, cakes, cookies and other pastries.

Mr. Henry was a short, stout man with white hair and a slight beard. He kind of reminded me of a very short Santa Claus. He walked with a slight waddle and always seemed to be out of breath. I think we bonded over being overweight.

"I brought you some cookies that Maisey made last night. Your favorite—chocolate chip," said Mr. Henry. He was smiling and he held the plate of cookies in his pudgy little hands. I stared at the plate of cookies. I could feel my willpower slipping away. Mrs. Henry, or Maisey, as he called her, made some of the best baked goods I have ever tasted. Chocolate chip cookies are my kryptonite. I really tried to say no, but the words would not form or come out of my mouth.

It was as if I had no self-control. It was like everything was in slow motion as I reached for the plate while smiling. I peeled back the cling film, picked up a cookie and took the biggest bite I could. I thought my head was going to explode. The sugar rush immediately surged through my body. I took another bite and noticed Mr. Henry standing there, smiling.

"Good, aren't they?" he asked.

I managed to swallow some of the cookie in my mouth and replied, "The best. Maisey is a pastry goddess," I shoved the rest of the cookie in my mouth.

"I'll leave the rest of them with you," Mr. Henry said. "She made at least five dozen last night, so plenty more for me at home. By the way, good work on the Anderson deal. Keep up the good work."

I watched him waddle out of my office and down the hall. I stared at the plate of cookies he left behind. I covered them back up with the cling film and put them into my side drawer.

"I won't eat you," I said, more like commanded. I felt a twinge of success and ate my second orange. I had the cookies beat. I felt pretty good, as if I was speaking for sugar addicts everywhere. I looked at the desk drawer and shook my head. I decided to bury myself in my work, and then, off to the boxing gym. My afternoon was set.

By 4:30 there were only three cookies left. I just couldn't stop eating them. And why, why God, did I have to eat all of them? What the hell is the matter with me? I felt so guilty and ashamed. I couldn't stop beating myself up. *You're a fat pig! I can't believe you ate the entire plate of cookies. It's a wonder you don't have diabetes. You are going to eat yourself to death. Some diet! You are worthless! Kryptonite.*

I didn't even take the stairs. I took the elevator and did the walk of self-shame to my car. I was still going to boxing class, but I felt terrible about myself and those stupid fucking amazing cookies.

****

As I drove home, I could not help but beat myself up about those stupid cookies. I called myself stupid, fat, ugly, a pig, unworthy, useless- the list went on. By the time I pulled into my driveway, I was so disgusted with myself, I wanted to curl up and die. I was so deep in self-loathing, that I didn't even notice Sabrina was on the porch in her workout clothes.

"Mom!" she yelled from the porch, "Hurry up, I don't want to be late for class!"

I nodded and waved to her. I had forgotten about the boxing class. Within seconds, I managed to gain some composure and get out of the car.

"I'm coming. Traffic," I said, a flat tone in my voice. I didn't even make eye contact with her. I walked past her into the house and went directly to my bedroom and shut the door. I could feel the tears swelling in my eyes. I don't know why but I prefer to cry alone. Part of me thinks crying is a sign of weakness, which I know isn't true. But nonetheless, I like to cry alone.

I slowly got dressed and went into the bathroom. I had forgotten about the scale, until I heard the voice.

"*So, a whole plate of cookies, Tubby? Not a good look. I hope you ate them in private. No one wants to see a pig eat,*" the scale cursed.

I wanted to reply, but what could I say? I believed the scale was right. I looked down at it and sighed. I gave it a swift kick with my foot, only to hurt my toes. I cried out in agony and limped out of the bathroom. I begrudgingly dressed in my workout clothes and followed Sabrina to the car.

"What's wrong, Mom? You look… I don't know, defeated," Sabrina said, not taking her eyes off the road.

"Yes, defeated! That is the perfect word. Defeated! I had a bad day at work, but I'm okay," I said, not wanting to admit out loud that I just ate almost a dozen cookies.

"Well, this workout will help you clear your mind. Working out is a great endorphin release. It's a natural high."

I listened to Sabrina talk about endorphins and stress relievers for the rest of the drive. I wanted to tell her to shut up, but I didn't. It wasn't her fault I had no willpower. By the time we reached the gym, Sabrina was pumped and ready to workout. I, however, was… what did she call me… yes, defeated. I just wanted to go home.

I reluctantly followed her into the gym. Soon, that dreamy instructor, Felix, appeared.

"Ladies, you came back! Let's get your hands wrapped," he said, clapping his hands enthusiastically. We followed Felix and went through the ritual hand-wrapping process, taking off our shoes and putting on boxing gloves. We, then, followed him and joined the rest of the class.

This class was pretty much like the first one, only this time we broke off into pairs. I thought Sabrina would be my other half, but a handsome young man asked her to be his partner, and she couldn't say no. The class had an uneven number of students, and I was left alone. I was actually okay with this and thought this may be a chance to sit down.

I was just about to turn and walk away until I heard a voice say, "Great, I guess this means we are partners." I turned around to see Felix smiling at me. Just my luck. The instructor is my partner. This day just keeps getting better.

"Oh, well…you know I'm not very good," I said.

"It doesn't matter. What matters is that you are here. Most people talk about working out, but to show up, well that's a big deal. Give yourself a point," his kind voice said. I can't lie, it made me feel slightly better.

As we went through the workout, I learned Felix really loves what he does. It wasn't so much the workout as it was teaching and helping people reach their fitness goals. The way he taught the class was actually very motivating. He didn't make me feel worthless or get annoyed when I was out of breath or slow. Instead, he would say things like, 'good job', or 'come on give me one more' or 'it's okay, we have all the time in the world'. He was encouraging, but tough.

I learned how to throw punches and kicks. We worked on form and the importance of the mind-body connection. I learned how to stabilize my fighting stance, and he even made me growl and roar to make sure I was breathing correctly. My mind was so busy taking in all the information, I completely lost track of time.

Before I knew it, class was over. I was winded and tired but felt good. I had almost forgotten about the ten cookies I had devoured earlier and thought I must have at least worked off five of them.

"You did really good for your second time. You are naturally strong and have good form. We just need to add a little bit of speed and power. That will come in time. I'm glad you are taking the class. How do you feel?" Felix asked.

"I feel better. I'll admit I didn't want to come, but my daughter was on my porch waiting for me. So here I am."

"I am happy to work with you outside of class. I'm always in the gym and could help you perfect your form."

Now, I know what you are thinking—enter the love interest right? How cliché do you think I am? Felix must have thought the same thing, but he followed up by saying, "I am a personal trainer, which is how I pay the rent. I'm not too expensive."

Now, I haven't been approached by many personal trainers, but I know that they do not come cheap.

"Thanks for the offer, but I probably cannot afford you," I said, still a little out of breath.

"Let's see what we can work out. I'll tell you what—the first session is free. If you like it, we can negotiate a fair price. Deal?"

He smiled and extended his hand to me. How could I not shake it?

"Okay, deal," I said while shaking his hand.

"Great. Our first session is tomorrow at 7pm since there is no class. Bring your gloves and a good attitude," he said.

I nodded and smiled at him. He returned the smile and walked away. He was cute, I can't lie. I was deep in my fantasy when Sabrina brought me back.

"So, I see you and Felix have become chummy-chummy, eh?"

"He is just looking to increase his personal training business. I have a free session tomorrow."

"Ooh a free session?" Sabrina replied.

"Yes, a free session. Sabrina, I'm sure that man is not interested in me, rather my wallet."

She laughed before dismissing me. "Whatever, Mom!"

Sabrina dropped me off and I was alone in the house. I was surprised that I wasn't hungry. But I was tired—no doubt about that. I decided to take a hot shower. Once I was showered and dressed in my pjs, I headed to the kitchen. I was going to stick with the diet. Today was just a minor setback. I made my lunch and prepped my breakfast. I was proud of myself for at least doing this much. What did Felix say, celebrate the little wins?

I was in the bathroom brushing my teeth when the scale spoke.

"So, day two was not as successful as we had hoped. Your kryptonite saw to that."

I spit out my toothpaste, "What the hell do you want from me?

"But since you are measuring your worth by what I say, and you fucked up royally today by eating all those cookies, I get to tell you the truth. You are fat, obese and if you want things to change, you need to back away from the cookies, Tubby. I don't want you stepping on me because I may not survive."

I didn't have a witty reply because deep down inside, I knew the scale was right. I am measuring my worth by the numbers that showed up when I stepped on the scale. I knew I fucked up today.

"I did workout."

"Okay, so you did a workout, big deal. One workout does not erase 100 pounds. You need more than one workout; you need a bunch of workouts, Tubby."

"Can you not refer to me as Tubby? It really doesn't help."

"Okay what do you prefer? Fatty? Big Girl? Hippo? Big Ums, Two Tons of Fun? Rollie Pollie?"

"Oh, you are hilarious."

"So, I guess for now we stick with Tubby, right Tubby?"

"Whatever. I'm going to bed."

"Night, Tubby."

As I lay in bed, I made three mental notes; 1. No more eating a whole plate of cookies; 2. Chocolate chip cookies are my kryptonite; 3. Avoid the scale before bed.

Chapter 6

The next morning, I woke up sore, but I felt pretty good. I thought about my workout with Felix and how I had forgotten about my day. Maybe there was some kind of power to working out. I was almost excited about going back to the gym tonight for my personal training session.

I managed to drag myself to the bathroom and shower. It was then when I stepped out of the shower that I heard that voice.

"Okay, Tubby, let's see where we are at?"

"Excuse me?"

"Step on me. Come on. You are dying to know if that workout session did any good. And I know you want to know if those cookies made a dent in the wrong direction. Come on, step on me."

I stood in my bathroom, dripping water on the floor. The scale was right, I did want to know if I had made any kind of impact. I knew it was only day three, but come on, three days should show something, right?

I walked over to the scale and looked at it. *It seemed harmless enough*, I told myself. It's just a scale, not a firing squad. I slowly put my foot on the scale, then the other. I didn't look down right away. I looked up at the ceiling and said a small prayer.

"Please, please, *please* let the number be a little less. Just a little. Please."

I looked down.

"Wow Tubby, you didn't lose, but you didn't gain. So maybe you can eat a plate of cookies and just be sure to hit the gym after. You keep this up, you will have made no progress. Pathetic!"

"Shut up!" I said while stepping off.

"Hey! No need to be touchy. I'm here to tell you the truth about your weight and the truth is you have made no progress in three days. Plain and simple. If you just stop now, we can hit the donut shop on the way to the office."

"Shut up, shut up, shut up!" I yelled. I picked up the scale and shoved it into the vanity cabinet. I didn't need this shit today. I wanted to cry but didn't. I was pretty much out of tears. Instead, I got mad. I decided I was going to show that scale I was in charge.

"The next time I step on you, I will be down five pounds."

The scale didn't reply. I felt like I had made a turning point in my mindset. I decided to get dressed, eat my breakfast, grab my lunch and head to the office.

****

Around 3pm, I got a call from Boonie. It was just perfect timing really as I needed a break anyway.

"Hey, girl. I'm sorry I've been out of touch. Tell me, how did you ever raise kids? Ivy is driving me crazy."

"Don't blame Ivy," I joked.

"Haha! Funny! So, how are you liking the boxing class?"

I smiled, "I knew you had something to do with it. I could tell Brina was acting funny. Not to mention she bought me all the equipment. You bought it, didn't you?"

"Guilty as charged. You seemed so down and I thought this would be good for you. So, tell me, do you like it?"

"I kinda do. I'm sore as hell, but I feel pretty good. I had my second-class last night. Felix is my instructor."

"Felix?"

"Yes, Felix."

"Ahh yeah… Brina told me you are getting some private Felix lessons. Girl, we signed you up for a class, but here you go making things private. That's why you my girl."

"Seriously, how often do you and Brina gossip about me?"

"Girl, please."

"It's strictly business. Besides, he says I'm naturally strong."

"Hmmm…"

"Not like that, damn Boonie, everything isn't about sex."

"But what if it was? You would be a lot less uptight; don't you think? Ain't nothing wrong with a lil' bump and grind after class."

"I'm not uptight."

"Girl, bye."

I heard the click in my ear and knew that this conversation would be continued later.

****

After work, I drove home, changed my clothes, and headed to the gym for a private lesson with Felix. As I entered the gym, I saw Felix and he waved to me. He always had a smile on his face. I wondered what his life was like. Did he have a family? Was he married? Kids? Girlfriend? I wanted to strangle Boonie for even putting a slight bump n' grind thought into my head. "Damn, Boonie!" I whispered.

I walked over to Felix. He was talking to a group of young kids. He motioned for me to have a seat nearby. I sat and listened to him speak to his class of youngsters.

"Okay, you guys did great today. I liked the hustle and the teamwork I saw. You are getting better and stronger every day. You should be proud of yourselves."

The kids smiled and gave one another high fives.

"As you know, I like to pick one member who has made amazing progress. You are all winners, but on different levels of ability. Nothing wrong with where you are at today, knowing you will be different tomorrow, and it's okay. So, you guys know the drill, who showed up and showed out today?"

The kids looked around then pointed to a little girl with red hair. She was a heavy-set girl with glasses. She was smiling.

"Steph, you get today's *Atta Girl* prize!"

I watched the team each stand in a circle and started clapping in unison. They began to chant, "Go Steph, Go Steph!" The chanting started out small, and then, got louder. Then, they each bowed to her and said one thing she did well in class. The little girl was smiling from ear to ear. She bowed to each of them as they praised her and gave each of them a high five. When they were done, Felix dismissed the class with these words, "Remember, we are here to better our minds and our bodies. Today, you honor me for showing up. Be the best you, you can be." The kids all bowed to him and the class was over.

I watched as the little redheaded girl ran to her dad, gave him a hug and high five. She was beaming, and even from across the room, I could feel how excited she was about being praised. Her father looked very proud and happy. It made me think about my days as a heavy-set child, trying to fit in and make friends. Our experiences were definitely worlds apart. I was so deep in thought that I didn't even realize Felix was standing next to me. He must have noticed me staring at the girl and her father.

"She did really well today. I'm glad the class picked her for the circle," he said, grabbing a pair of gloves. "I didn't know if you were going to show up or not, but I'm glad you are here. Ready to get to work?"

"I am," I said, trying to mentally convince myself that I was ready.

"Great. Today, we are going to get into the ring and work on form."

"The ring?"

Felix laughed, "Yes, the ring. It's okay, it's just you and me."

I nodded and began the ritual of wrapping my hands. I was getting pretty good for only day three. When I was done, I grabbed my boxing gloves and walked over to the ring. Felix was already inside holding a pair of sparring pads. I took a deep breath and pushed myself in between the ring ropes. I had never been inside a boxing ring. I looked around. *Nowhere to run,* I thought to myself.

For the next 90 minutes, we worked on form, power, how to stand correctly, how to throw a hook, jab, uppercut, right cross, left cross, elbows and body blows. He showed me how to duck punches and move from side to side. We worked on footwork and how to move back and forth. I was slow but was getting the moves down pretty well. I was winded fifteen minutes into the 90-minute session but stuck with it. I was actually having fun and enjoying the motions.

Felix was kind and patient. He never got frustrated when I had to stop for water or to take a breath. He always gave me positive feedback and took the time to show me my mistakes. By the end, I was drenched in sweat, but felt really good. For the first time in a long time, I felt like I had accomplished something. I was proud of myself, which isn't something I have felt for a very long time.

When I finally stepped out of the ring, my legs were shaky. I was ready to sit down, when Felix said, "No sitting. Now, it's time for pushups and sit-ups. I'm going to need 50 of each."

I shot him a confused look. Was he being serious? But he responded with a smile and nodded his head. I don't think I have ever done 50 pushups or sit-ups in my whole entire life. I was afraid if I lied on the floor, I wouldn't get back up. I slowly made my way down to the floor.

"You look worried?" Felix said. "You can do the pushups on your knees. Over time we will work up to full push up. Go ahead get started."

I lay flat on my stomach and raised my upper body, leaving my knees on the floor mat. I slowly came down and then back up.

"One," Felix said, "Only 49 more to go. Don't worry, I got no place to be."

I closed my eyes and did another pushup, then another one. I did this over and over, fighting the sensation in my arms and abs. I could feel sweat dripping off the edge of my nose. I wanted to stop, but I didn't, I just kept lowering and raising myself back up. I had to stop at every eighth one, but I managed to make it to 50.

"Nice job, now on your back and do 50 sit-ups," Felix said.

I groaned and slowly rolled over on my back. I bent my knees and put my hands behind my head. I slowly began to raise myself up, then back down. I closed my eyes and counted. I had to stop at every sixth sit-up, but I did it! I made it to 50. Felix bent down and gave me a high five.

"You did it! But I knew you could."

"I'm glad… one of us knew… it. I… wasn't so sure… I was gonna m…ake it," I said, while panting. I was still on my back and wondered how I was going to get up.

"Well, tomorrow is group class. I hope to see you."

"You will. I'm actually starting to like this. Maybe one day I'll get in the ring and fight."

Felix looked at me and smiled. "And I will be in your corner cheering you on. However, we have a way to go before that happens. So, let's just take it slow, okay?"

I nodded and slowly stood up. He gave me another high five and walked away. I had made it to 90 minutes. *Not bad,* I told myself, *not bad at all.*

As I was driving home, my stomach growled. It dawned on me that I hadn't eaten anything since lunch. My first instinct was to drive directly to *Burger, Burger, Burger,* but I could hear the scale mocking me. So, I decided to stop at the grocery store and pick up items to make a salad. This was completely out of my character. In the past, a salad was not a meal, but a side dish—a way to offset whatever unhealthy food I was putting in my mouth. The salad was there so I could say, *See, I eat vegetables.* Then, I would drown it in ranch dressing.

This time would be different. The salad would be the meal—what a concept! I walked into the store, grabbed a shopping cart and went directly to the produce section. I picked up spinach, leaf lettuce, cucumbers, tomatoes, mushrooms, and carrots. I went to the condiment section and got low-fat balsamic dressing. I thought about croutons but decided against it.

As I was walking to the checkout, I passed the bakery section. My eyes ravished the brownies, cakes, cookies, and pies. I slowed down but didn't stop. I wanted to stop; I really did. I almost did, until I heard the scale voice in my head, *"Go ahead Tubby, eat another dozen cookies. You did workout really hard today. Another day of no progress. Pathetic, Tubby!"*

I hurried away from the bakery and went directly to the checkout line. I purchased my rabbit food and left the store. *I am in charge, not that fucking scale,* I told myself. I started the car and headed home to make my salad.

Chapter 7

By now, you are probably thinking that all I do is go to work, eat, and recently started going to the gym. Not true. I do actually have a life—I have friends, you already know Boonie, a great career and even some hobbies. I consider myself to be average. I mean, I don't have the perfect Instagram life, but I do have a life.

I raised my kids and sent them off into the world. I had no idea my husband, now ex-husband, would decide to venture out with them, but he did. I was proud that I didn't curl up and die because Lord knows I wanted to. It is hard when you dedicate your life to your family, and one day, they are gone——doing great things, and living great lives.

If I have to be honest, it was probably five years prior to the divorce that I really started eating a lot. I was alone most of the time and food was a great comfort to me. That's about the time I started dating the *Burger, Burger, Burger* spot too.

After the divorce, to keep myself busy and to stop myself from eating into oblivion, I joined a book club. It was fun at first, but then it turned into a *whine* club and I wish I meant the drinking kind. After the book club, I tried volunteering at the animal shelter. I really enjoyed it, but I couldn't handle it when they euthanized the animals. I was getting too attached. By the time I left I had three cats and four dogs. I have re-homed all of them, but for a while, my kids thought I was turning into the crazy cat lady.

My oldest son suggested I volunteer with people not pets. He directed me to a small nursing home that was looking for volunteers to visit, read and spend time with the residents. At first, I wasn't all that gung-ho on the idea. I mean, I had been taking care of people for the better part of my life. Do I really want to spend my time with old people? My son then replied, "Mom, you are old… in a good way of course." That was enough to push me to prove him wrong. So, I did.

Overtime, I truly found myself wanting to go and sit with Doris, the feisty Jewish lady who always tried to get me to marry her son. Or Walter, the ex-schoolteacher who always had a book for me to read. Or Marsha and Stanley, married for sixty-five years and would spend hours showing me photos of their past adventures. But it was Frank who I think made the biggest impression on me. He was heavy, like me, and had so many health problems because of his weight, but he always had a smile on his face. I felt like I could be me with Frank, and he never said anything about how or what I ate. It was like the male version of me—only white and much older.

Frank had been heavy all his life. He said he just liked food too damn much. He thought about losing weight, but the idea never took hold, as he put it. He could barely walk, coming in at almost 500 pounds. He had to have a special bed, shower and all of his clothes were specially ordered for him. He married young in life and had a daughter, but he never saw her. His wife couldn't deal with the weight gain. He said that she always felt like she was competing with food. He said that food was his wife, mistress and comfort. I remember one day he told me that if he had to do it all over again, he might make better choices when it came to food.

"I let food control my life. It had become a friend who was always there to comfort me in my time of need," he said one day when we were out taking a walk. His breathing was labored and his steps were short. He slowly pushed the walker in front of him and took another step.

"There is still time for you. Don't end up like this—big, fat, and unhealthy. It's no way to end a life."

"You are still here, Frank," I said, "Still here walking and talking."

"For now, but one day this will all become too much."

"But not today," I said.

We continued to walk a few more steps until he finally decided to sit down at a nearby chair. He slowly positioned himself over the chair and let himself down. He let out a heavy sigh, took out a handkerchief and wiped the sweat from his brow.

"How far was that today? Had to be at least 40 steps" he said, slightly winded.

"Hmmm, maybe more like fifteen," I told him.

"Well only 35 more to go," he said while smiling. "So, what you been up to? I haven't seen much of you lately."

"Well, I joined a boxing gym and started working out. I've only been a handful of times, but I'm really starting to like it."

"A boxing gym?"

"Yes, Frank, a boxing gym."

"Now, I never figured you'd be the fighting type."

"I'm not… not really anyway."

"You could have used some of those moves to kick your old man's ass!" he laughed, which soon morphed into heavy coughing.

"Are you alright?" I said, patting him on the back.

"Oh, I'm fine. So, you tryin' to lose some weight?"

"Not trying, doing. I went to the doctor and she called me obese."

Frank howled with laughter.

"Obese? Is that what it took to push you over the edge? I've been obese all my life and I don't think anyone, besides a few doctors, have ever said so."

"Well, it pushed me to look at myself. So yes, I'm losing weight."

"You on some fancy diet? I saw something about a diet where all you eat are keys. Now, I don't know why anyone would want to eat keys."

"Keys… wait! Frank, it's called Keto and you don't eat keys."

"Then, why the hell call it Keto?"

"I don't know, Frank."

"So, what special diet food are you eatin' anyway? Does this mean you won't bring me anymore of the *Burger, Burger, Burger* food? And don't try to bring me no goddamn salads!"

Frank was a kind and gentle soul, but most people cringed at the sight of him. He had so many health issues; diabetes, high blood pressure, high cholesterol, breathing and respiratory issues, and last month, he had a bad case of gout. He had issues getting dressed and undressed, walking and sleeping. He had a distinct odor and only showered a few times a week.

The first time I met him, I found myself gagging at the sight of him. The smell coming out of his room was almost unbearable. During my first couple of visits to the home, I avoided him altogether. I was, and I hate to admit, disgusted at the sight of him.

One day, I was walking by his room and overheard a conversation he was having with his daughter. I was told she didn't come to visit often and when she did, it usually ended up in an argument. This visit was no different. I shouldn't have listened, but honestly, I just couldn't help myself.

"Dad, I'm not coming up here anymore. All you do is eat and sit in this room. I'm embarrassed. You should be embarrassed. Look at you?! Look at this room?! It's disgusting!"

"No one asked you to come up here. I'm fine. I don't need you coming up here telling me what to do. If you gave a flying fuck, you would have never put me in here in the first place."

"I can't do this anymore, Dad. I can't. You are an embarrassment."

"Is that why I never see my grandkids because I'm an embarrassment? My size bothers you? I raised you. Worked two or three jobs to make sure you didn't go without. I worked hard and long hours. When your mother died, I felt like I had lost everything. I wanted to die too. So, I ate. I tried to eat myself to death. But the more I ate, the less I thought about your mom and being alone. Food became my joy and comfort. Then, I broke my hip and couldn't work anymore, so not only was I eating all the time, but I also wasn't moving anymore. I don't need you being embarrassed for, or about me. Just get out. Get the fuck out!"

I heard a crashing noise, followed by a scream. I immediately ran into the room and found Frank on the floor. He had fallen out of his recliner when he was trying to get up.

"Dad! Let me help you." His daughter ran over and tried to lift him, but it was useless. She looked up at me, "Help me!" she screamed.

I rushed over and tried to help lift Frank off of the floor. The smell of his body was unbearable. Finally, a couple of male orderlies came into the room. All four of us were able to finally lift Frank back into his recliner. We were all out of breath and stood looking at one another for a moment. It was Frank who broke the silence.

"Thank you. I'm not sure what happened."

He was staring directly at me. Sadness washed over me. I could relate to what he had said about his wife and food.

"I'm leaving, Dad... this is too much." I watched as his daughter grabbed her purse and stormed out of the room.

I stayed as the orderlies did a quick check and then left. "Are you okay?" I asked.

"I'm good, I suppose. Nothing broken. I don't see the ground often, but when I do, I know it isn't a good thing. I'm Frank. I've seen you around visiting the residents. I see you reading, laughing, and talking with them. Wondered why you never made it to my room."

I didn't know what to say. I had been avoiding him.

"I'm sorry. I…"

"I know the smell is not too good in here. I'm not stupid."

"No, it's not that, I just…"

"It's okay. Could you push that walker a little closer? I promised the doc I would try and walk every day. I guess now is as good of a time as any."

I pushed the walker closer and watched as he pushed the remote-control button and controlled his chair. The chair rose up, basically standing for him. When he was all the way up and standing, he took a step forward.

"Care to join me? I never walk too far."

That was how we became friends. I realized that it is so easy to judge someone on how they look and not realize there is a story behind all the mess.

We talked that entire afternoon. He told me all about his life and happier times. We talked about our weight and how it had snowballed out of control for both of us. He understood what I was going through, and I understood him. I was proud to call him my friend.

I would visit Frank as often as I could during the week, and on the weekends. I really enjoyed the time we spent together.

"Us fatties have to stick together," he would always say to me. "It's a myth that fat people are jolly. Whoever came up with that shit is a fucking idiot! I'm not jolly! I'm in pain most of the time. I can barely breathe, and taking a shower is a major event in my life. Jolly my ass! Are you jolly?"

"No, I'm not and who are you calling fat?"

"Look, you can be honest with me. I'm fat. I know that it has a stigma. My own daughter wants nothing to do with me because of my size. But I've come to terms with my weight. It's you that struggles with that label."

I wasn't as comfortable with my weight as Frank was. He had given up. He had no desire to lose weight and often said it would be food that would kill him.

One day, I decided it was time to clean Frank's room. The smell was horrible. I mopped and scrubbed every corner of the room. I asked the nursing assistants to help me change his bedsheets and made sure that they were changed every week or more often if necessary. We made a deal that he would shower every other day, as opposed to whenever he felt like it. I brought scented candles and those outlet deodorizers to help keep the room smelling good. I even did his laundry. By the time I was done, you wouldn't recognize his room. I have never seen him cry, but he did that day.

"No one has done something so nice for me in a very long time," he said. I watched as the tears rolled down his cheeks.

"Stop or we will both end up crying," I managed to say, even though my voice was cracking. But it was too late. We both sat in his room, bawling our eyes out. We both promised to never bring it up again.

<u>Chapter 8</u>

After three or four months, going to the gym had become a habit. I was getting better and stronger. I was feeling really good about my commitment. I hadn't touched or been near the scale. It was where I had left it in the vanity cabinet. I wasn't sure how much weight I had lost, but I was feeling better about myself. I had been watching what I was eating and managing my portions.

Things were going pretty well. I came home feeling great from my latest boxing class. The soreness had gone away, and I could see tiny changes in my body. I decided it was time to get on the scale. Full of confidence, I walked into my bathroom. I hadn't heard the voice of the scale in a while, and I was sure I had beaten whatever craziness I had had.

I opened the vanity cabinet and pulled out the scale. I carefully set in on the floor, *You won't be calling me Tubby this time*, I thought to myself. According to all the research I had done on weight loss, you shouldn't weigh yourself at night. I guess your body is lighter in the morning. But I didn't care—I was stepping on that scale.

I took off all of my clothes and stood naked while staring down at the scale. I wasn't really comfortable with my body and I rarely looked at it in the mirror. I glanced at my naked body in the mirror, then down at the scale. When I lifted my foot to step on the scale, I heard the voice.

"I knew you would be back," the scale said.

I didn't respond. I placed my left foot on the scale, then the right. I didn't look down, instead I looked up and said a little prayer.

"Please let the number be smaller. Please be less. Please."

I held my breath and looked down.

"Tubby, you've made progress. You are down fifteen pounds. Good job, Tubby."

All I could do was grin. I was down fifteen pounds. I weighed 260 pounds.

"Now tubs, if you listen to me, you could lose more. You know I'm your friend. I can help you."

"By calling me, Tubby?" I snapped back.

"No, no. By helping you measure your worth. These numbers mean everything. I can change your life. If you agree to step on me every day, I will show you a new you—a better you. No more locked away in the cabinet. Whatdya say… friends?"

"How do you measure my worth?"

"Everyone knows that when the numbers on the scale get smaller, life gets better. Thin is in. Think what you could do if you weighed 210 or 200 pounds. I mean that's thin for you but that's beside the point. I can help you get there."

"How? You are a scale."

"Yes, I'm a scale. I am the tool that from now on, you will use to measure your worth. The numbers I reveal are important. Everything you do will be for those numbers. These are the most important numbers of your life. Just think how your life will be when you are thinner. Dare I say, skinny? Your life will improve. Your drab non-existent love life needs improvement. You can stop hiding at the old folk's home and hang out with people your age—have a social life. Everyone knows skinny, thinner women are more popular, beautiful and have more fun. Everyone wants that."

I slowly stepped off the scale and grabbed a towel to wrap around my naked body. I had to admit, the scale was making a lot of sense.

"I have to step on you every day?"

"To keep you honest and focused. Come on, Tubby. I promise I won't call you Tubby anymore."

I sat on the edge of the tub staring at the scale. I did want the numbers to keep getting smaller. I didn't have a love life or social life for that matter. By becoming thinner, the self-loathing will stop. I will have more confidence. I can start dating again, buy new clothes, go shopping. I could go on a beach vacation and wear—dare I say it, a two-piece. I would be worthy enough to be in a relationship. I would be more likeable, and maybe I could ditch the old folk's home for a group dating thing or something. I would be someone my love interest would be proud to have on their arm. My kids would stop pestering me about losing weight and I could prove my ex wrong. When I lose weight, I will be worthy of everything I want. The scale had my full attention.

"Okay. I will do this," I said. "No more calling me Tubby."

"Deal! No more Tubby."

I had made a deal with the scale. For the first time in a long time, I felt that things were changing for the better.

The next morning, I woke up earlier than usual. I had started walking two to three miles before work. Felix had suggested running, but my bad knees would never go for that, so I walked instead. When I returned from my walk, I went directly to the bathroom and stepped on the scale.

The scale had actually gone down by two pounds.

"See, Tubby… I mean see, Chubs… Your worth."

I smiled and stepped off. I did feel a little more worthy after that reveal.

"Two pounds. I'm on a roll!"

I quickly showered and dressed for work. I ate a light breakfast and packed a nice salad for lunch with several pieces of fruit and a baggie of baby carrots.

All day, the words that the scale said to me bounced around in my mind. *Worthy!* Did being thinner really make one more worthy? I was deep in thought when Stephanie, my assistant, entered my office. Stephanie was a thin girl—probably weighed no more than 110 pounds. She had long black hair and wore very little makeup. I once overheard the other assistant classify her as frumpy. I liked

Stephanie. She was very smart and basically a mind reader, which is what we all want in an assistant.

"The presentation is in your email. I reformatted it and used PowerPoint."

"Thanks, Stephanie!" She turned to leave the office, but I called her back. "Hey Stephanie, any plans this weekend?"

She turned around and answered, "No, not really. You?"

"No, just the gym, if that can be classified as plans."

"The gym? I'm impressed. You seem to be going more. You look great."

"Thanks. I feel better, but I have more work to do. Need to be *worthy* before I buy new clothes."

"Worthy? That's a strange way of putting it? Why do you want to be worthy to buy new clothes?"

"Did I say worthy? I meant thinner. Thinner before I buy new clothes. You probably have no issues in that department. You can basically wear whatever you want."

"I guess. Sometimes I see something nice on the rack and try it on, and it doesn't fit right. Being skinny doesn't mean sexy. Curves are sexy. I don't have curves like you. Curvy women are lucky."

"You think so?"

"I know so. Men like curves. My brothers, uncles, and ex-boyfriends have all said so. I think women dress for other women. I don't think men really care. Anyway, I've got that report to finish. Do you need anything else?"

I shook my head no and watched her leave. I had never really thought of myself as curvy—round yes, curvy no.

****

After work, I drove straight to the gym, I had stopped going home first about six weeks ago. I was getting pretty good with my form. Once inside, I wrapped my hands and went directly to a heavy bag. I put on my gloves and started punching the bag.

Felix had told me to focus on my breathing and to use my legs for power. I moved around the bag and punched. I threw combinations and even some kicks. I was feeling pretty powerful when Andy, the other trainer approached me.

"Hey, you're getting pretty good."

"Thanks!" I replied., continuing to throw combinations as he watched.

"Hey, have you ever thought of getting in the ring and maybe fighting? You have the power. You just need to drop a little more weight."

I stopped punching.

"Me? No, I don't think I need to invite an ass whooping."

"I could train you. I know you work with Felix, but it may be time to kick it up a notch. I can see that you have lost about ten pounds…"

"Fifteen," I said, correcting him.

"Okay, fifteen pounds. You work with me and I can get you to lose another 20 to 25 pounds in three to four months. We can build muscle and put you in the ring. We do Friday night fights here twice a month. It's all amateurs, but a great way to access your skills and get some real action."

"Andy, right?" He nodded in response. "I've seen the people you train and I'm no fighter. I'm here for the workout. Besides, I'm way too old to be fighting anyone."

"Age is simply a number. Think about it. We could start next week. I'm sure Felix would encourage you. You have to challenge yourself and step out of that comfort zone. Do things you thought you never would. You could win. There is no money involved, but you get a little trophy and bragging rights. Of course, you would fight other girls. Anyway, think about it."

I watched Andy walk away. Me, a fighter? I've seen those girls he was referring to. They get in the ring and want to take someone's head off. They are younger, hungrier, faster, and want it way more than I do, but it would be great to lose another 25 pounds in three to four months. Maybe it was time to kick it up a notch. I decided that I would ask Felix what he thought after class.

When class was over, I pulled Felix aside.

"Felix, I want to ask you a question." I was nervous and didn't know why. "Andy approached me today about fighting in the Friday night fights, what do you think?"

As usual, he smiled before he spoke, "Really? I never pegged you for a fighter."

"I know right, but Andy said I have the power. He did say that I would need to lose about 25 pounds, but he could help with that. He would train me."

"Well, Andy is a great trainer, but he is serious about the art. He is no nonsense and demands a lot from his fighters. His training never ends. It is a mindset—not only the physical stuff, but you have to be prepared mentally as well."

"Do you think I could do it?"

"I think you can do whatever you put your mind to, but your body has been through some trauma. You said you have a bad back and wonky knees. It may not be worth it. I can help you lose weight if that is what this is about. I also worry about your age. The girls Andy trains are much younger than you. Now, I'm not saying that you are old, but these girls aren't even 25."

"I know, I thought about that too. But it's not like it's a real fight, right? Just a trophy and bragging rights."

"You could get seriously hurt."

For the first time, Felix was not smiling. His face was stern and serious.

"You are not ready. You've been doing this what, three months? I'm glad you are getting in shape and feeling better about yourself, but fighting is something different. You are not ready, and you also need to lose more weight."

"I know, Felix. I got that part. I know I will lose weight. I really thought you would support me on this."

"I don't want to see you get hurt because you are trying to prove a point. I think you are doing great with the progress you are making. Can't you be happy with that?"

"I'm not trying to prove a point Felix. I think I can do it and want your support."

"Well, I'm sorry. I think it's a mistake. It's not worth getting hurt—like seriously hurt. Too many bad things can happen because of your age, and body. I would encourage you to take Andy's class to challenge yourself, but I don't think getting in the ring with a 22-year-old is smart."

"My age? My body? Thanks for the vote of confidence, Felix. Andy thinks I have potential."

"After everything I just said to you, all you heard was the stuff about your weight and your body? Seriously? You have to be smart. Do what you want, but I won't support you fighting."

Felix walked away without giving me time to reply. I was hurt. I really thought he would support me on this. Now I felt like I did have a point to make. I was going for it. I was going to train with Andy and fight in the Friday night fights.

Before I left the gym, I found Andy and told him I was in. I would start training with him next week. He said we needed to focus on my weight and it wouldn't be easy. I told him I was up for it. This old lady was about to prove all her doubters wrong.

Chapter 9

I had lunch with Boonie a few days later. I really hadn't seen much of him and he was not pleased with my excuses or stalling tactics. We finally decided to have dinner and drinks at our local spot. The food was good and the drinks were cheap.

I got there first—Boonie was always late. I think he did it on purpose to make some kind of dramatic entrance. I was sitting in a corner booth when I saw him walk in. He looked around and spotted me. I watched him walk towards me. He looked tired, which is unusual for Boonie. He prided himself on his youthful look and upbeat personality.

As he got close to the booth, I stood up and turned around for him. He stopped dead in his tracks and exclaimed, "OH MY JESUS! GURL!"

"I know right, down a little over fifteen pounds!"

He hugged me and we both sat down.

"I can't believe how good you look! See I told you that gym would do wonders."

"I'll admit, at first I really hated it. I was always out of breath and tired, but I stuck with it."

"Well honey, it is a good look on you! I like it. I'm so proud of you. It's good to see you doing something else other than going to that depressing nursing home. I mean, I know it's for a good cause, but honey, that Frank was becoming your best friend."

"What the hell does that mean? The man is lonely—he has no one."

"Well, don't get mad. I mean, damn girl—you and Frank were regulars at the *Burger, Burger, Burger* spot. You know I will always be straight with you. You also know that I love you, so I will just say it, that man is not good for you. He has you eating as much as he does. Keep it up and you'll be just like him—trying to walk and need a small crane to hoist you into the tub. And I know I only met him once, but the smell that was coming off him was too much, honey… too much." Boonie held up his hand in front of his nose and waved it back and forth.

I sat back and shook my head, "Yeah, I know. But I do have some exciting news. I'm going to fight in the Friday night fights at the gym. I should be ready in about four months. I start training in a few days."

His jaw slightly ajar, Boonie looked at me as if I had grown a third head.

"I never thought I would see you speechless," I said.

"What do you mean, you're going to fight?"

"You know, get in the ring with another person. They try and hit me, and I try and hit them. A fight, Boonie."

"Why in the hell would you want to fight? Girl, you are too old to be getting into anybody's ring. Have you lost your mind? I need a drink. Where is the waiter?"

"What do you mean too old?"

"You know exactly what I mean. What is wrong with you? I think trying to lose weight has gone to your head."

"I really thought you would support me on this."

"Honey, I have supported you through three kids, one husband, a marriage, divorce, numerous jobs, and whatever else came up. I have known you most of your life, but this *thing* you are talking about is just fuckin crazy, okay? You think I would support your getting in a boxing ring and fighting someone, seriously?"

"I'm not crazy. I'm going to train, drop an additional 20 to 30 pounds and fight. I think you would hate to see me thin and happy. At least when I was fatter and depressed, I was available to you all the time. But now that I've started working out and not being so available, this is what I get from you?"

"What are you talking about?"

"Every time I get something of my own, you have to talk shit about it. When I got married, you talked shit. Told me he was no good and all this other shit. You talked shit about all three of my pregnancies, my divorce, and my career choices. When I volunteered at the animal shelter, you talked shit. When I started volunteering at the nursing home, you talked shit. You know what, I think I can become a good fighter. I really don't care if you support me or not. I finally see what you really think of me. I might be a little slow on the uptake, but I got it now."

"What the fuck are you talking about? You are losing it."

I stood up. "Whatever Boonie! I'm out. Thanks for your fucking support." I turned my back to him and hurried out of the restaurant.

I had never fought like that with Boonie before. I walked out onto the sidewalk and started walking towards my car. I could hear Boonie behind me calling my name, but I didn't turn around. I needed his support and all he did was talk shit. I didn't need him. I was done. I was starting a whole new life myself.

I was changing. I had read somewhere that as you evolve and grow, sometimes you have to leave some of your friends, even family, behind. They may not be on board with the changes you are making in your life. Sometimes you have to ditch your old mentality, and that may include people. Maybe it was time for me to dump Boonie.

The drive home was long. I was furious that Boonie did not support me, and I never knew he felt the way he did about Frank.

When I got home, I went into the bathroom, completely undressed, and stared at the scale.

"Okay… From here on out, the numbers are just going to get smaller." I said out loud.

I stepped on the scale and looked down at the numbers.

"Okay, fat ass it looks like you gained a couple of pounds from yesterday. You probably spent your entire day thinking about food."

"It's only a few pounds. Monday, I start serious training for my amateur fight."

"Well fatty, time to get serious."

"You and me are going to be really good friends. I will prove my worth. Once I lose the weight, most of my problems will disappear. You'll see."

I stepped off the scale and got dressed.

****

Monday finally arrived and it was to be my first day of training with Andy. I spent the workday in my office, looking through reports and trying to keep myself focused. I had no idea what to expect. I had seen Andy's class, but never really paid much attention.

About 3:30 pm, Sabrina called me. I hadn't really spoken to her lately and I hid out all weekend, not answering my phone.

"Mom, where have you been? I've been trying to reach you all weekend."

"I've been around. What's up?"

"Are you going to class tonight?"

"I am, but I'm not taking Felix's class anymore."

"What do you mean? You are doing so well. You look great. What else are you doing?"

I paused and prepared myself for her reaction.

"I started training with Andy. I'm going to fight in the Friday night fights."

"What? What do you mean?"

"I mean get in the ring and fight."

"Mom have you lost your mind? You are too old to be fighting. Have you seen the girls Andy trains? They are no fucking joke, Mom. You've lost it!"

"I haven't lost it, Sabrina. Andy thinks I have potential. I start training today. Once I lose another 20 to 30 pounds, I can and *will* fight. And I'm not that old. Why does everyone keep saying that?"

"Mom, those girls are all of 22 or 23 years old, maybe younger. You are 50-something. Most of them have been training for years. I don't want to see you get hurt. Why are you doing this? What did Felix say?"

"You know what, I guess it was too much to ask my family and friends to support me on this. I'm a grown ass woman who can make her own decisions. You, Boonie and Felix can just stay out of it."

"Wait, so Boonie and Felix aren't feeling this either?"

"Look Sabrina, if you don't want to support me, then don't. I'm hanging up now."

I quickly canceled the call. Fuck, why can't anyone be on my side? I'm not too old. Am I? Okay so I'm not in the best of shape, but that is all about to change. I will train, get stronger and prove everyone wrong.

I thought about Sabrina's words as I drove to the gym. I did have flashes of doubt, but I was going to do this. When I arrived, I found Andy standing near the ring.

"Hey, I'm here. I'm ready."

"Good!"

"Should I wrap my hands?"

"Nope. We start with road work—cardio. I don't care how strong you are, without good cardio, there is no fight. Then, learning and perfecting combos, bag work, shadow-boxing, sparring, and fight technique. You need to run three to five miles, three to four times a week. This includes sprints to help with speed. We will do two nights of normal class, one night of sparring class and forty-five minutes with light weights or floor conditioning. This is not Felix's class… *This* is something else. I would advise you to buy a better pair of running shoes, too."

"I didn't realize it was so intense," those were the only words I could muster up after listening to him.

"It is. Everyone is outside. We are running today. Put your stuff away and let's go."

I slowly walked away and put my stuff in an empty locker. As I turned, I noticed Sabrina walking in. We made eye contact, but she quickly turned away. I joined Andy and went out the back door where the rest of his class was waiting.

"Okay everyone," Andy started, "You know the drill if you are only running three miles, turn back at the park, if you are running five, turn at the small ice cream store on Taylor Avenue. Be sure to keep your time and hydrate. Let's go."

Everyone was smiling and nodding their heads. I felt so out of place. I started running.

I started out slow and was the last one. I checked my watch and tried to find some kind of pace or rhythm. My breathing started out even, but after about ten minutes, it had become more labored and jagged. I knew I should be breathing in through my nose and out of my mouth, but I just couldn't make it work. I could feel sweat beading on my forehead, and I was starting to develop a cramp on my side.

My run started to change into a jog, but I kept going. I tried to control my breathing but couldn't find a rhythm. To add to it, my chest and lungs ached. I wanted to stop. Just when I thought it could not get any worse, I could see Andy running towards me. This meant, he had made it the 3 or 5 miles and was running back to the gym.

He didn't even look at me, he just ran past as if he didn't know me. I looked up again to see the entire class quickly approaching. I watched they one by one. No one made eye contact with me. They just ran by.

After about 30-40 minutes, I rounded the corner to the gym's parking lot. I thought my legs were going to collapse at any moment. I slowed my pace and leaned against a car. I bent forward, trying to control my breathing. I took several deep breaths until I could get a rhythm. I felt a wave of nausea come over me. I quickly leaned forward and vomited. After a few minutes, I felt better, but still winded.

Andy was waiting for me by the back door. He looked at his watch and shook his head, "We need to work on your time. Class isn't over. Time for combo and bag work," Andy said. He waited as I composed myself and walked into the gym.

The next part of the class was brutal. We did three and four punch combinations with kicks and knees. We broke off into pairs. One person would hold pads, while the other did the combinations. We worked on three-to-five-minute timers.

I was paired with Paige. A young 20-something beast of a woman. She had rock hard abs, muscle-y legs and her arms were like small cannons. I held the pads for her first. Her first punch pushed me back into a nearby pole. I felt the pain shoot down my back. She motioned for me to move forward and hold up the pads. She punched and kicked for what seemed like an eternity. I could feel the force of her punches send waves through my hands, shoulders, and arms. This woman was powerful.

At the end of her five-minute round, the bell finally rang. I slumped forward feeling as if I had just had the shit kicked out of me. My legs and arms felt like rubber. We were told to switch. I put the gloves on and she wore the pads. Andy said because I was new, I could do three minutes. It was the longest three minutes of my life.

I was grateful that Paige had pads on because she came at with full force. She forced me to punch and duck. She moved me around the floor and backed me into corners. She forced me to keep my hands up or get bashed on the head with a pad. She was relentless—no breaks, no breathers. I threw combination after combination. I kicked and blocked. When the ten second warning bell rang, I dropped my hands. I thought she would back off, but I was sadly mistaken. The minute I dropped my hands to my chest, she launched the pad into my right cheek. The force of her punch knocked me to the ground. I was shaken and surprised at the same time. At that moment, the bell rang. Three minutes was up!

"Never put your hands down. Never," Paige said and walked away.

I sat there for a moment watching her walk away. Had I bitten off more than I was willing to chew? I was thinking about quitting when Andy approached me.

"Hey, you did okay. Paige is tough, don't let her demeanor bother you. She is like that with everyone." He held out his hand and helped me to my feet. "The workout isn't over. You are training to fight. This isn't Felix's class. You have another 90 minutes."

Was he kidding, 90 fucking minutes? I was sure I wouldn't make it. The rest of the class consisted of more combination rounds, heavy bag work, jump rope, and shadowing boxing. I hated every minute of it, but I made it through the first day of training.

I slowly made my way to the car and drove home. I was exhausted and feeling crushed. The right side of my face hurt, and my knees were aching. When I arrived home, I went directly into the bathroom and started to run the water for a bath. Andy had suggested I soak in Epsom salt and hot water. He said I would be sore and instructed me to drink plenty of water. He also gave me an extreme diet to follow. What did I get myself into?

After a long hot bath, I started feeling a little better. It took a minute to get out of the tub, but when I did, I decided to weigh myself.

I slowly stepped on the scale and didn't look down. I just looked up at the ceiling trying to muster the courage to look down.

"What are you afraid of? Look down. Come on fatty, just look, you may be surprised."

I sighed and looked down. I was surprised. I had lost two pounds.

"Yea!" I screamed.

"See tubs, you lost two pounds. Today, you are worthy."

At that moment, I decided to continue to train to fight and to really commit to Andy's diet. It was the best two pounds I had ever lost!

I walked over to the bed and laid down. Before long, I fell asleep.

****

Chapter 10

The next six months were a blur, and was the beginning of my downward spiral. I was becoming someone else. And even though I was losing weight and getting in shape, I had become fanatical. I ran every day. I was up to about three miles without stopping, and I followed the fighter diet Andy gave me. The diet consisted of high fiber vegetables, fruit, lots of smoothies, water, water and *more water*, protein powder or tuna or chicken, and absolutely no carbs.

In the beginning, was hard. I mean *hard, hard, hard*. The first week I went to *Burger, Burger, Burger* twice. I was doing the training, but had lost all confidence after the first day. I wanted to quit, but now I had something to prove. I mean, who gets their ass kicked during a pad workout?

I went back the next day. I think everyone was surprised to see me. My respect points increased and even Paige began to work with me instead of against me. We actually became friends. We started hanging out. We ran and worked out. She shared some dieting tricks and taught me about protein powders and other supplements.

Paige was young and judgmental. She despised anyone who didn't care about their body. She couldn't understand how anyone could just eat and eat without thinking about the effects on their body. I remember the conversation we had during training one day. We were hitting the heavy bag. I was probably down about 35 pounds and looking pretty good, or so I thought.

Paige was leaning up against the bag holding it for me when she said, "Doesn't it bother you that you're fat? How can you stand it? I mean, I'm not trying to be rude, but how? I don't get it?"

I stopped punching and looked at her. Did this girl really just body shame me? I was a little stunned and it took me a moment before I answered her.

"Paige, I'm sure everyone has a reason—good or bad—for doing the things they do. This includes those of us who are overweight and overeat. I do not speak for everyone, but I will tell you this. As a person who has struggled with weight all my life, I don't need you to be my mirror. I know what I look like. I know I'm overweight. I don't need you to tell me. I tell myself every day. As a matter of fact, I avoid mirrors because I can't stand the image staring back at me."

I didn't give her a chance to answer. I walked away from the bag, leaving her to think about what I said. We never mentioned it again.

I began to resent those around me who did not get on board with my new life. I was finally doing something about my weight, but no one seemed happy for me. I was all in on this—there was no alternative for me. I had committed to fighting. Though I had my own doubts, I never once said anything to anyone.

I avoided my co-workers and didn't attend office functions like birthday parties or baby showers. As much as it hurt me, I had to tell my boss to stop bringing me his wife's amazing cookies. I could see the hurt in his eyes, but I was on a mission. I stopped having lunch with the rest of the staff, too. I never visited the café anymore and rarely left my office. If I did, it was to go on a run. I never thought I would be saying that.

I visited Frank less frequently. I found it difficult to visit him. He always wanted me to bring *Burger, Burger, Burger* or some other kind of fast food. I found myself resenting his attitude toward my desire to lose weight. Because I stopped visiting so often, Frank reverted back to his old habits of not bathing or getting out of bed on a regular basis. When I would visit, I found myself thinking about how disgusting he was. I felt as if I was better than him because I was losing weight. I would make excuses to leave early or not come by at all. I tried calling, but he stopped taking my calls. After a while, I just stopped seeing him altogether.

I had received a call from the other residents that the nursing home was making Frank leave. The facility could no longer care for him and the residents complained about the smell coming from his room. I thought about going to see him but didn't. A decision I would come to later regret.

Boonie and I haven't spoken since that day in the restaurant. We could both be very stubborn, but I wasn't going to give in this time. I did call him once and he sent me directly to voicemail. Now, when your bestie sends your ass to voicemail and you know that you have been sent to voicemail… well, it doesn't feel nice. I left him one message. It was not good.

Something like, "Fuck you Boonie! I don't need your sorry ass in my life anyway. This is how you do a friend? Wow! Okay, I see what's up, that how you want it—fuck you, Boonie!"

My kids were even worse. They tried to have some kind of intervention. I should have known something was up, because they all showed up on a Sunday and brought dinner with them. Which was even more unusual because none of them cooked.

I found out later, they had decided to take matters into their own hands and stop me from fighting. My kids have always been close. Marcel had always looked out for Zaire and Sabrina, and he could be a little overprotective.

Sabrina had reached out to her brothers the moment she found out I was fighting. They had dismissed the idea and told her that I would change my mind once the training got difficult. When this didn't happen, Sabrina called them again, this time demanding they meet in person and do something to stop me.

Once they were all at Marcel's place, they began to formulate a plan.

"Mom is really losing her mind," Sabrina said. "I thought we would join a gym, lose some weight. I didn't think she'd go crazy and want to fight."

"She's not gonna fight," Marcel said. "I'm no expert, but I'm sure the training is brutal. Mom is not old… but she's older. She'll stop once things really heat up."

"I don't think so," Sabrina said. "She is really acting strange. I think she is determined. Like she is trying to prove something."

"You'd think you two would be happy she is doing something," Zaire interjected, handing each of them a beer.

"Something is off," Sabrina said. "Mom isn't even speaking to Uncle Boonie. He called me. He said they had a fight. He said mom left him in the restaurant when he said he wouldn't support her fighting."

"Yeah, that is strange, Boonie and Mom don't fight," Marcel said, taking some time to mull over what Sabrina had said.

"Okay, so what do you propose we do?" Marcel asked. "You're the genius who took her to a boxing gym," he said looking at Sabrina, "Why not a regular gym? Why a boxing gym?"

"This is not my fault," Sabrina said, taking a swig of her beer.

"Is she any good?" Zaire asked.

"I don't know. I haven't really seen much of her. All I know is that she's training."

"Maybe we can get Dad to talk to her," Zaire suggested.

"Are you crazy? Why you trying to set Dad up, Zaire? You know Mom would go off. Especially if she's learning how to fight," Marcel said.

"Just a thought," Zaire replied.

"What makes you think Mom would even speak to Dad. I don't think that they've spoken to one another in a long time. Ever since Jamaica, things were never the same between them. I always wanted to ask Mom what happened, but I never did," Sabrina said.

They sat in silence while drinking their beers. It was Marcel who came up with a plan.

"Intervention," he said.

"What?" Sabrina and Zaire said in unison.

"Intervention. We have an intervention. We can do it over dinner. Wait… I got it! We can make her dinner. We can bring it to her house; it will be a surprise! Mom likes surprises, right?"

Sabrina and Zaire both shook their heads no.

"Mom hates surprises. Do you remember that time we tried to give her that surprise birthday party? She was not happy," Zaire said.

"Okay, but this is different. It's us. She says she never sees us, and we never come over for dinner. So, let's have dinner at her house. We can cook and everything!" Marcel said, sounding very pleased with his plan.

"Cook? Who is cooking?" Sabrina said.

"We are. We can get Boonie to help us. We can do like chicken and potatoes. It will be good. She will be so happy to see all of us—she won't see it coming. It's perfect."

"I don't know, Marcel. Mom isn't stupid," Zaire said.

"It's not about her being stupid—it's about catching her off guard. She'll be so happy to see us and the dinner we brought her. Come on! It's the perfect plan. Then, once we get dinner started and she is relaxed, we talk about her fight. We tell her how much we love her and tell her she is too old to fight."

"Uh, wait, you gonna tell Mom she is too old?" Sabrina asked. "I know you got a doctorate an all, but that just sounds like some dumb shit."

Marcel looked at her. He knew she was right. The mom he knew had not been meek when they were growing up. She had been the disciplinarian in the house, making sure all the kids stayed in line. She had been strict, but fair, and she was always one step ahead of any of their plans, plots or clever schemes.

"Okay, so maybe I don't… I mean… we don't mention her age. We all know it's true. I'm not saying Mom is old, but getting in a boxing ring with a 30-year-old…"

Sabrina quickly corrected him, "20-something-year-old."

"Even worse, a 20-something-year-old girl is just madness. I think she is having a mid-life crisis."

"What is a mid-life crisis?" Zaire asked.

Sabrina smiled, "I got this. A mid-life crisis is different for women than men. You see, when a man has a mid-life crisis, he goes and buys the sports car or gets a hot young girlfriend. These things make him feel young again. But for a woman, a new car or hot young guy isn't enough. We seek beauty and acceptance because society tells us old women are ugly and undesirable. So, we seek to recapture our youth physically. Look at how many older women have plastic surgery compared to men."

"So, Mom is doing this to be younger?" Zaire asked, sounding confused.

"No, Mom is trying to recapture her youthful body, hence the working out. How many times have either of you mentioned her weight to her? Once, twice? I know that it bothers her, but she was so busy with us, it left little time for herself. Hell, even dad bounced when she starting gaining weight. I'm not saying they didn't have other problems, but y'all know Dad is vain. Look at him now with Patricia. She is a fucking barbie doll compared to Mom. All I'm saying is that I think Mom is trying to recapture a young, youthful body. A new sports car or young hot boyfriend wouldn't be enough. She wants to feel better about herself."

They all looked at one another. Each of them was guilty of telling their mom about her weight gain. It wasn't done out of malice, but rather out of love. Sometimes, when you get criticism from those who are closest to you, it can be hard to tell the difference.

"Maybe if we approach her with love, she will listen," Zaire said earnestly.

"Such a mama's boy," Marcel said.

"You're just mad because she loves me the most," Zaire joked.

"You're the baby, and everyone knows the baby always gets spoiled." Sabrina laughed.

"Well, baby or not, we are not approaching her with love. She needs to listen to reason. I will take the lead. What else do you know, Bri?" Marcel returned the conversation to the task at hand.

"Well, I know that she is training, a lot. I don't go to class that often anymore, but I know the fighting class is two to three hours a night. They run and do all kinds of shit. It's crazy."

"Mom is working out two to three hours a night?" Zaire exclaimed. "That's bad ass. I think it's kinda cool. Mom probably gets in the ring and kicks some ass!" Zaire started doing fake karate moves around the kitchen.

Marcel and Sabrina watched him for a moment. "Okay, knock it off Bruce Lee," Marcel said. "This is serious. Mom could get seriously hurt Zaire. We need to go over there, on a Sunday, bring dinner and have a serious talk. An intervention is much needed."

"I think we should tell her we are coming," Sabrina said.

"No, this will catch her totally off guard. She won't see it coming. We will have the advantage," Marcel said while smiling.

"Y'all really gonna go to Mom's house and tell her she is too old to fight and she is not fighting?" Zaire asked.

"Yes," Marcel said. "She will listen to reason."

Zaire and Sabrina looked at one another and decided that they would follow Marcel's lead. Marcel was always in charge of his brother and sister when they were kids, making decisions for them, and keeping them in order. They decided what to have for dinner and who would bring what. Marcel felt confident that his plan wouldn't fail.

The day of the great *"stop mom fighting intervention,* I was out running. When I approached my yard, I noticed all the cars parked in front of the house. Sabrina was sitting on the porch. Next to her was a larger roaster pot. My youngest son Zaire was on his phone, leaning up against his car. He had a couple of bags of groceries on the ground next to him. My oldest son, Marcel, was standing on the porch, pacing back and forth.

They were surprised to see me running. I ignored their expressions and ran up the porch and checked my time.

"Mom?" Sabrina said, "You've been running?"

I could see the look of shock on her face when she saw me. I was almost 40 pounds lighter and was looking rather spectacular.

"Yes, Sabrina, I run. You know I'm training." I retrieved the house keys from my pocket and unlocked the door. Sabrina, Zaire, and Marcel followed, carrying their bags of food and the large roaster.

"So, what's all this?" I asked. "I've never known any of you to cook."

They all looked at one another. It was Marcel who spoke first.

"We are worried about you, Mom… with this fighting business. It's crazy talk. Not saying that you are crazy, but you are a little old to be fighting, don't you think? We think this is some mid-life crisis. You have been pretty down since you and Dad divorced."

He was looking sternly at me, as if he was my parent and I was his child. I started to speak when Zaire jumped in.

"Look Mom, we know it's hard to start over again, but Marcel is right. This fighting thing is really crazy. You could get hurt."

I looked at Sabrina to see if she had anything to add… she did.

"Come on Mom. I know I was the one who talked you into the class, but now you have taken it to a whole new level. Fighting? I've seen these girls and they are no joke."

I stared at their worried faces, annoyance boiling to the surface.

"Listen you three, I don't go inserting myself into your lives. I'm glad you care about me and I love you all for it, but I am committed to this. I am preparing myself both physically and mentally. What I don't need is you putting doubts in my head. I need support, and encouragement. If you can't do that, then I'm going to have to ask you to leave, until this is finished. I have been training for six months. My fight is in three months. If you can't get with my program, then you need to leave." I tried to maintain a calm and level tone, even though I was seething in anger.

"Leave?" Sabrina asked.

"Yes, leave. What'll y'all call it... haters? I don't need haters right now."

"Haters?" Marcel interjected. "We ain't haters, Mom. We care about you. What are you doing? This has got to stop, and it stops now!" His voice was raised as he stood over me. I think he forgot who he was talking to. I stood up.

"Listen, all of you. I'm the mama, not you, you or you, but me. I'm a grown and can do exactly as I please. I don't need this from any of you. It's not a mid-life crisis or whatever else you may think. But what you are not going to do is come into my house and tell me what is what. Have y'all lost your ever-loving minds? And I want to thank each of you for the vote of confidence! If you don't like what I am doing then get the hell out and take your food with you. I ain't eating that shit anyway!" I walked over to the front door and opened it. "You can take your amateur intervention and get the hell out of my house. Don't bother saying another word."

They each looked at me in disbelief. I had never thrown my kids out or spoken to them in the manner, but I had had it with all the doubt I was getting from everyone in my life—my kids, Boonie, co-workers, and even Frank. It was too much.

Slowly, each of them began to make their way to the door. Zaire tried to speak, but I cut him off. I didn't want to hear anything else. "I really thought my children would support me on this. I've supported you three your entire lives. I don't ask for much, do I? I've been unhappy for a long time, and now that I found something for me, this is what I get from you."

They filed out of the house one by one, each wore a look of surprise and disbelief on their faces. Sabrina was the last one out the door. She turned to me, still holding onto her roaster. "Mom, you've really lost it. We care about you. We love you. We don't want to see you get hurt."

I stared at her. I knew they meant well, but I wasn't thinking like myself. I had turned into someone else. I was fanatical about my dieting and exercising. I was starting to lose control, but I wasn't ready to admit that to anyone, especially the kids.

I didn't reply to her. I just shook my head and slowly shut the door. I watched them through the window, all huddled together. The conversation seemed to get heated with arms flying upward and wild hand gestures. Finally, they all got into their separate cars and drove away.

I went into the bathroom and stared at the scale. We had become good friends over the past several months. The words had gotten kinder and the scale praised my efforts. I became excited to weigh myself daily. Every day, the number had become smaller, and the scale would give me praise.

The scale had stopped calling me tubby or tubs. I was relieved. I had gone from 275 to 235 pounds in about six months. I was wearing a size fourteen or sixteen and felt pretty good about myself. I knew that with the weight falling off, my life would surely change for the better.

I stepped onto the scale.

"Hello old friend, the only one who gets me," I said out loud.

I watched as the scale registered 233 pounds.

"Good job. No more Tubby for you. You are becoming more worthy every day. Thin is in, and you are here to win."

"Winning is the name of the game, alright!"

"See, once you start losing weight, life gets better. I've been here for you the whole time. I have never left and never let you down. I'm on your side."

"At least someone is," I said while stepping off the scale.

"You haven't hit your goal yet, so we need to up your training and decrease food intake. Trust me. The next time you step on me, the number will be smaller. See, everyone liked you fat and complacent, but now you are something else. They are just jealous."

I shook my head in agreement. I had the fight of my life in just 3 short months and Andy said I had to be at 200 pounds to fight.

What was an additional 35 pounds? I heard the scale whisper.

I could do it. I could increase the number of times I ran, try to add more miles, could work out twice a day and supplement food with protein shakes or smoothies.

I stared at myself in the mirror. I wasn't sure if I liked what I saw. I mean, I liked losing the weight, but it felt like I had lost my family and best friend too. *They're just jealous,* I thought to myself. The scale was right—they are jealous.

Jealousy is a funny emotion. It doesn't allow you to think straight or rationally. It can drive you to madness. I have felt such jealousy and madness at the end of my marriage. I would like to say that it was all his fault and I was just a victim, but that just isn't true.

I walked into the bedroom and went to the big walk-in closet. At the top of the closet was a large box filled with pictures I had taken over the past years—school pictures, family pictures, vacation, birthdays and so on. I retrieved the box and dumped the contents onto the bed—so many memories. I sat down and started looking at the pictures.

They were pictures of the kids in school, team photos, and photos of a Christmas years ago. I smiled as all the memories passed through my mind. Suddenly, I came across of picture that was taken about six years ago. It was just before the divorce. The family had taken a vacation to celebrate Marcel's doctorate degree. He had decided he wanted to go to Jamaica. It was the last family vacation we took. I was standing while holding a drink, smiling and waving. You would think I was happy, but I wasn't.

I remember that feeling of jealousy then. I was jealous that Carl was doing whatever he wanted. That he was never home and always working late. I wasn't at my heaviest weight then, but just over 240 pounds. We had been on the island for about two days. Carl and I had not been getting along. He was always taking jabs at me because of my weight gain. The kids didn't know we had been sleeping in separate rooms at home, and Carl had started staying out late. He said it was work, but I knew differently.

We fought constantly. The more we fought, the more I ate. The more I ate, the more we fought It was a vicious circle.

The day the picture was taken, we were on our way to a horseback ride activity. I'm not sure who picked this outing, but I promised myself I would try and have a good time. The bus was packed with about 20 people who had chosen to horseback ride. I sat behind two blonde women on the bus. They were talking about riding horses. I tried not to listen, but I couldn't help myself when I heard one of them mention a weight requirement.

"I'm so excited we are doing this. This will be my first time on a horse," one of the blonde ladies stated.

"Me too. I haven't ridden in a long time. My cousin, Amy, did this same excursion last year, and she said they weighed her before she got on the horse."

"What? Are you serious? They weighed her? Why?" The other lady asked.

"She said it was because she was heavy-set."

"Did she get to ride?"

"She did. She said the weight max was 240 pounds. She said the embarrassing thing was that they weighed her in front of everyone. Could you imagine stepping on the scale and everyone seeing your weight or knowing that you weigh over 240 pounds if you can't ride."

I felt my stomach drop. I was sure I weighed more than 240 pounds, but I didn't say anything. Carl was busy chatting with a young couple, Marcel and Zaire were deep in conversation and Sabrina had taken up with young man who was also on vacation with his family. I sat there wanting to run, but I was trapped.

Once at the facility, we were led into a lobby. We were given waivers to sign to absolve the place for any injuries. As we broke into groups, our guide approached. He was a loud boisterous Jamaican man. He took one look at me and spoke loudly.

"We need to weigh you! You may be too big to ride today! How much you weigh darlin'?" His Jamaican accent was thick.

The room became a little quieter than before. There was still some chattering, but almost everyone in the room stopped when they heard the man's comment. I wanted to die that very moment. I have no words for the amount of shame and guilt that I felt at that moment. I didn't answer him. I'm sure it was only a brief moment, but it felt like an eternity. Carl broke the silence.

"There's a weight requirement?" Carl asked, looking at me with that look he always gave me when my weight became an issue. "Did you know this?" he said, still looking at me.

"Yes, sir. Our horses can only take so much!" The boisterous man howled with laughter. "Come on darlin' I have a scale over here." The man reached for me, but I took a step back.

"I'm okay. I really didn't want to ride anyway," I said. I wanted to look at Carl, but I just couldn't bring myself to look in his direction. "I can wait here and take the next van back to the resort. I'll be fine."

"Are ya sure, darlin?" the man asked.

"Yes, I'm sure. I'll be fine. You guys go ahead, I'll meet you back at the resort."

"Are you sure, Mom? I'll stay with you?" Zaire said.

"Or I can," Sabrina said. "We can go to the spa."

"No, I know you really wanted to ride, so go ahead. We have three more days here. I'll be fine. I can use some downtime anyway."

Carl didn't offer to stay or say anything. He just had that look on his face—a look of disgust. I would become accustomed to this look during our divorce.

Later that night, once everyone was back from riding and was getting ready for dinner, Carl approached me about the horse-riding situation.

"Why didn't you let him weigh you?" He asked. The tone of sarcasm hung in the air. "Do you weigh more than 240 pounds?"

"And what if I do, Carl?" I asked.

"Really? If you do, then you need to do something. You are so fat that you can't even ride a horse! A horse! That's just fucking embarrassing. I'm embarrassed. You embarrassed your family today. Your fat ass embarrassed us again!"

"Again? Just how long have you been embarrassed by my fat ass?" I screamed back.

"You just don't get it. You think you look good? You think I want to be married to a fat, overweight cow? You are not the same person who I married. At least back then you weren't obese. And don't try and blame it on the kids or your job like you always do. I met you in the fucking ice cream aisle. I should have known then; you eat because you have no fucking self-control."

I wanted to tell him I ate because of how I felt about myself. I wasn't happy. I wanted to lose weight, but it just felt hopeless, so I kept eating. I know it sounds crazy, but he was right—I just couldn't help myself.

"I'm done," he said.

"What do you mean by that?" I asked, sounding panicked.

"I'm done. I don't want to be married to you anymore. I don't love you. I'm not sure if I ever did."

"What?"

"You were pregnant."

"What do you mean Carl? We had two more after that, and now you tell me that you never loved me? I don't look so good to you now? I raised your kids, and you did the honorable thing, and now it's time for you to go? You don't love me because I'm fat? You vain motherfucker! I can't believe I'm hearing this right now."

"Why did you marry me?" he asked.

"Because I thought I loved you and you loved me, not because I was pregnant. And now, I find out the truth after all these years."

"I'm leaving when we get back home. I had planned to tell you then and not spoil the vacation, but I guess it doesn't really matter now, does it?"

"I guess it doesn't," I responded.

That was the last real conversation I had with my ex-husband. He might have stuck around if I hadn't ballooned to 240 pounds, but in the end, he never really loved me anyway.

Divorce wasn't enough to send me into a dieting frenzy; in fact, it did the opposite.

Upon arrival home from our Jamaican vacation, Carl, true to his word, moved out and filed for divorce.

It was at this time that I began to eat my emotions. I constantly ate because it was a great comfort to me. It was as if the 'I'm full' switch didn't work in my brain. There were nights where I would eat from the time I got home until I went to bed. I formed a habit where I always had dessert before going to bed. I fell into a 'that is fat girl shit' phase and ate in bed every night. Sometimes I would wake up with plates or bowls in the bed. *It really is some fat girl shit*, I told myself one morning, as I rolled off of a spoon.

Food had become my best friend. Which is funny, because in the past, when I was on some diet, I would fear food. Now, it was my bestie. It didn't take much for me to turn to my bestie for comfort. If I received a letter from Carl's attorney demanding whatever, I ate. If I had a fight with Boonie, I ate. If I felt sad or depressed, I ate. Food was the only thing that gave me a false sense of comfort. I could curl up with some ice cream or brownies and eat myself to a false bliss. Of course, this feeling didn't last very long and was always fleeting. Once the joy began to fade, the self-loathing barreled its way through.

You are your biggest critic, and it doesn't matter what anyone else thinks about you. When I looked in a mirror, which was rarely, the negative chatter in my head went wild. I more critical of myself than Carl ever was. I thought I looked hideous. That is the energy I carried with me and it was exhausting. I told myself I was a cow, fat, ugly, undesirable. Who would want to be with you? You were too fat to ride a horse! Your husband left you because you are fat, and the list goes on and on. At this time, I was a victim of my own shit. I couldn't blame Carl or the kids for my weight—it was all me.

Now, as I stand in the mirror looking at my transformation, I wondered what Carl would think. Would I be good enough for him now? I weigh less than I did then. I stood in the mirror and turned sideways. I sucked in my gut and stuck out my butt, "Not too shabby," I said out loud. I started to feel a little better about myself. The scale was right; I was becoming worthy. Fuck Carl!

Chapter 11

I doubled my runs and trained in the morning, as well as at night. I had joined a second gym, so I could focus on weight and strength training. All I did was train. I had no social life and didn't want one. I was too focused on my goal.

I did venture out once before the fight. Andy was having a birthday party at a local bar. There would be food, karaoke, dancing, pool and darts. I really didn't want to go, but Andy asked, and I couldn't say no. I had gotten rid of many of my old size 20-something clothes and now had a closet of size fourteen to sixteen clothes. I can't lie, it felt good.

I had purchased a really cute low-cut black halter top and a pair of size fourteen jeans. When I put these clothes on, I transformed into someone else. For starters, I could see my feet when I looked down. I didn't have to cover anything up with a sweater or jacket. I had lost weight in my chest—yes, a real thing—and the girls were looking great. My face had thinned out too.

Though, I still had the underarm flab, I put my arm in the "show your muscles pose" and wiggled the fat back and forth. I almost changed my mind about the halter top, but then I thought about it. *Who cares? You look good.* I completed the outfit with a strappy pair of heels.

I gazed at myself in the full-length mirror. It was strange, I looked thinner, but I still saw the fat me gazing back. I blinked my eyes a couple of times and looked again. This time I did see a thinner me. My first instinct was to call Boonie. He was the perfect fashion consultant. I missed him. We still hadn't spoken in months. I had never gone this long without talking to him. I wondered if he missed me. I looked for a moment longer, did a single twirl and blew myself a kiss. I practiced smiling and saying, "Nice to meet you", a few times in the mirror. I was ready.

I drove to the bar with my confidence on full gear. Shopping for clothes was something I never really enjoyed, but buying this outfit did wonders for me that night. I pulled up in the parking lot, parked, and turned off the ignition. I took a few deep breaths, retouched my lipstick, and went inside.

The bar was brightly lit, and pretty crowded. I spotted Andy toward the back of the bar, near the pool tables. I made eye contact and he waived for me to come join them. As I made my way through the crowd, I thought I might be the oldest person in the place. There were plenty of 20 and 30 somethings talking, laughing, drinking, and eating. After what seemed like an eternity trying to wade through the young crowd, I made it to Andy and his party.

As I walked up to Andy, it was clear that he had been drinking heavily. He kind of swayed in a small circle as he stood. He held a beer in one hand and a shot of something in the other hand. He had a goofy smile on his face and greeted me by holding up both hands and saying, "You made it!" The words came out a little slurred, but you could still understand him.

"Hi, Andy!"

"You actually came! I didn't think you would," he said, stepping out of the circle and staggering towards me.

"Why wouldn't I come?"

"Well, you are so much older than my friends. I just didn't know." He swayed back and forth trying not to spill his shot. "Hey, do you wanna shot? I got everything—tequila, vodka, gin, beer, wine. That's funny, you want a shot of wine, that might be more your speed." He laughed at his joke and took his shot, chasing it with a long gulp of beer. Someone called his name and he turned and staggered away. I was looking around the place when someone tapped me on the shoulder.

"Can I get you something from the bar?"

"A glass of Moscato please," I replied to the waitress. She turned and left.

I was standing alone when a somewhat drunk Paige walked up to me.

"I… so surprised you came. I mean you are kinda *old*," she said. She also swayed back and forth. These people can really drink.

"I'm not that old Paige," I said dryly.

"Well, you need to catch up with the rest of us!"

"I'm good. The waitress is bringing me a glass of wine."

"Wine? Who fuckin drinks wine anyway? No one drinks wine. Old ladies drink wine… my mom and grandma drink wine. You need a real fucking drink… a shot."

"No Paige, I'm training. A glass of wine is fine for me."

"Training? Oh yeah, training. Well, I gotta tell ya, I didn't think you would make it this far. I mean, even though you have lost weight, you are still a fatty. I mean, look at you… what are those size sixteen jeans or something like that? Double digits equal fatty. I know how you fatties like to try and dress and be like us skinny girls, but really, it's just kinda sad. Oh, I know Andy says you are doing good, and you are." At this point she grabbed my face and shook it back and forth. "But honestly, me and other girls thought that Andy was playing a prank on us. We have a bet to see who is going to kick your ass in a few months. But no worries, if I win the bet, I will go easy on you. Can't say the same for the other two girls, but I like you. You got heart and a lot of ass! When you fall on it, it won't be that painful. Cushion baby cushion!" She howled with laughter at her joke. "I need another drink!" And with that she staggered away.

At that moment, the waitress came and handed me my glass of wine. I took it from her hands. I stood there feeling like the joke of the day. My training was a joke to Paige and others. I wanted to ask Andy if my training was a joke to him too, but instead, I gulped the entire glass of wine and left without paying.

I sat in my car, trying to hold back the tears. I could not believe what just happened to me. I reached out to put the keys in the ignition to start the car when someone knocked on my passenger window. It was Felix. I rolled the window down.

"Hey, you okay?"

"I'm okay."

He stood there for a moment, then said, "Let's talk for a moment, catch up. Maybe I could sit with you?"

I unlocked the door. Felix slid into the passenger seat and closed the door. There was an awkward moment of silence, then he spoke.

"You really look good. I saw you inside. I almost didn't recognize you."

"Thanks," I said, still trying to hold back my tears.

"You okay?"

"Oh yeah, I'm just fucking great." The tears started to flow down my cheeks. "Paige told me that everyone thinks my training is a joke. Do you know how hard I have worked? I have starved myself. I train before and after work. I run daily. I have basically told my friends and family to fuck off because they think this is a joke! This is my life!"

I buried my face in my hands. I felt Felix put his hand on my shoulder.

"You know, I think what you have accomplished is amazing. It really is. I think you have set high goals for yourself and you are reaching them. But... I think you lack balance in your life."

"Balance? What the fuck are you talking about, Felix?"

"I'm talking about balance. What good does it do to lose all the weight and not be healthy? Starving yourself isn't healthy, training constantly isn't healthy, cutting friends and family out of your life isn't healthy. Health is more than just weight. Health is all things. How do you feel? Do you feel good about yourself?"

I looked at him. I didn't understand what he meant. I had always thought that losing weight would solve all my problems, not create them. He continued to talk.

"I was happy to see you the first day you came to my class. I could tell that you were ready to make some changes in your life, and I was honored that you had chosen my class to help with that change. You were making great progress and taking slow steps, which is okay. We never had the opportunity to talk about nutrition and the idea of not dieting but making lifestyle changes. You look good. You've lost about what, 30 pounds?"

"Almost 45…" I corrected.

"Wow! Congrats! But what happens when the fight is over, and you start eating regularly again? Or you cut back on your training? Do you plan on living the rest of your life like this?"

I hadn't even thought about what he was saying. Training and losing weight so that I could fight was all I thought about.

"No," I said.

"Like I said, no balance. When you live a balanced life, you give time and energy to things that build you up, make you happy and give you life. Spiritually and emotionally. You can't give everything to one area of your life and be happy. Your balance isn't the same as mine, but you have to find it. When I said you weren't ready to fight, I meant you weren't ready because you had no balance."

He took my hand and gave it a squeeze.

"I think you are a pretty amazing lady. I do wish you well in your fight. I will be there for you when you do fight. Good luck with the rest of your training. Kick some ass! But more importantly, find some balance in your life. I'm gonna go now. Take care."

He opened the car door and left. For a few minutes, I sat there thinking about what he had said before starting the car and pulling out of the parking lot. I drove home in silence. I didn't even turn the radio on. I thought about what Felix had said about balance. I never thought about it before. I honestly thought that if I lost weight, the rest of my life would fall into place, but it would seem the opposite has happened.

As I drove, I passed *Burger, Burger, Burger.* I thought about stopping. It was my go-to place when I was feeling down. A good burger, fries and large chocolate shake always made me feel better. But I didn't stop and drove straight home.

Once inside, I decided to call it a night. I didn't know if I would sleep or not because my mind was racing. I went into the bathroom. The scale was there, staring at me intently. Oh, I know it didn't have eyes, but it was as if I could feel it staring at me.

Since I started this journey, the scale was the only consistent thing in my life. I stripped down to my underwear and stepped on it.

"I see you are back for some love. You've gained two pounds. What's that about? We need to be going the other way. What the fuck is your problem? Do you like being fat and keep in mind, you are still fat," the scale said.

"I don't need this," I said stepping off the scale.

"You can run, but I never lie. You had better lessen your food intake if you want praise from me. I'm the one that got you here. It was me who showed you how to be worthy. You just want to eat burgers and brownies. You want to lie to yourself, but I won't let you lie. I'm your best friend. Your only friend."

I knew the scale was right because, at that moment, it was my only friend. I was going to finish what I started, which wasn't my M.O. I usually start things; they get hard and I stop. I had to finish. I had to prove to myself that my training was not a joke—it was real.

The next morning, I got up for my run. I forgot about Felix's speech about trying to find a balance. My mind dwelled on Paige's words. Three months to fight night and I would prove them all wrong. Joke or no joke, I was determined to see this through.

Chapter 12

In the next twelve weeks, I trained harder than I had ever imagined. I lost an additional 45 pounds during that time. I was losing about four to five pounds a week. I had pretty much stopped eating regular food and drank most of my meals. In hindsight, it wasn't healthy, but it was effective.

I devoted all my drive and energy to training. I was losing weight rapidly, and though I looked amazing, I still didn't feel good inside. I hadn't even considered dating—any kind of love life wasn't even on my radar. I had all but sworn off love after my divorce. I was married to a man who said he really never loved me. He married me because I was pregnant. I can see where Boonie's ex-wife would have issues with him being gay. It's almost the same thing—we both married men who did not love us, they married us because we were pregnant.

I did date one guy during all this madness and obsession. I think if I would have been in the right frame of mind, it may have worked. His name was Marc. I met him one day while I was out running.

Later when I would tell this story, Boonie would call it a meet-cute.

I was running one morning. I was deep in thought about my training and didn't see him or his dog. I tripped over the dog's leash and hit the ground with a thump. I was more angry than bruised, I usually ran in the morning to *avoid* people and their dogs. He helped me up and was truly apologetic.

What can I say about Marc? He was tall, almost six feet and bald. He had rugged facial features and his skin was a beautiful soft brown color. His voice was deep, yet gentle. He had a nice body, too—not too big like that of a weightlifter, but you could tell he took care of himself. As he stretched his hand to help me up, I noticed he did not have a wedding ring.

As I stood, his brown lab circled me, and I got more entangled with the leash. We both started laughing and that seemed to break the ice.

"I'm sorry. I have just started walking him. He is new to the leash."

I smiled as I untangled myself, and just for the moment, I let down my guard.

"No worries. I wasn't paying attention. It was my fault too." I stepped out of the leash and was free of the dog. I smiled at him and bent down to pet the dog.

"What's his name?"

"Bossco," Marc said proudly.

"Well, Bossco, with practice you will get better," I petted and stroked Bossco. I didn't realize that Marc had been watching me the entire time. I stood up to find him staring at me. It was a little awkward, but Marc had a way of making me feel at ease.

"My name is Marc." He smiled and held out his hand. That was it. That was our meet-cute. We talked a little more and he asked for my number. Without too much thought, I gave it to him. I really didn't think he would call. What I liked the most about the moment, is that he was attracted to me. It had been a long time since a man actually spoke to me and showed interest. It was flattering. I floated on cloud nine for the rest of the morning, and well into the afternoon.

That night I trained for two and a half hours and was home by 9:00 pm. It had been my routine: come home, shower and make my lunch and prep my breakfast for the next morning. I didn't watch TV anymore because I had started listening to podcasts about weight loss, diet tips, training and fighting. I had completely emerged myself into this obsession.

I was about to put on one of my podcasts when my cell phone rang. My phone never rang because the kids and Boonie had stopped calling. The ringing had startled me as I stared at the phone number on the screen. I didn't recognize the number, but I answered.

"Hello?"

"Hi, this is Marc. Am I catching you at a good time?"

I felt a little flutter in my stomach. "Hi, Marc. Yes, this is a good time. How are you?"

We talked for over two hours, covering everything from religion to politics.

I learned he was around my age, divorced, two grown sons who lived in another state, and he was a chef. I told him that I was going to fight, and he seemed to be impressed. Not that that is the reason why I told him. I told him because I knew I wasn't available to date. I spent most of my time training.

After a couple of weeks, we found ourselves in a routine. He would call every night and we would spend hours on the phone. He came to my office for lunch and would bring me gourmet lunches from his restaurant. He didn't own it, but he was the head chef. I didn't eat most of what he brought me, because I had mostly been drinking my meals. I never told him, but I think he suspected.

Another month passed, and we got closer. I can honestly say that I was falling in love with Marc. He never mentioned my weight or size. It just didn't seem to matter to him. When I would celebrate losing another two or three pounds, he would say things like; *you look good now, why do you want to be so skinny? Why are you fighting? What is the purpose?*

I would try and explain it to him, but he just never understood why losing weight was so important to me. I couldn't tell him that once I lost the weight, all my problems would be solved. I also couldn't tell him I had a talking bathroom scale, who had become my best friend. I couldn't tell him that the scale measured my worth and weight.

One night, I invited Marc to come over. I hadn't slept with him yet. I was uneasy about letting anyone see me naked. I had a hard time looking at myself—what would he think? We had fooled around—mostly PG stuff. Every time we were close to having sex, I would call it off and pull away.

We had planned a dinner/movie night. Well, Marc would eat dinner and I would drink mine or have a light salad. My eating habits had started to bother him. It wasn't long before he realized I really didn't eat.

He arrived promptly at 7:30pm. I had forgone training to spend the evening with Marc, lying to Andy that I had to work. When I opened the door for him, he had four large bags in his hand. I let him in and directed him to the kitchen.

I helped him unpack the bags. He had candles, wine, chocolate-covered strawberries, two beautiful steaks, baked potatoes, salad, salad dressing, and for dessert double chocolate chip cookies. The ones that come in a pan all by themselves. My emotions were all over the place—I was annoyed and happy at the same time.

"I hope you don't mind; I picked the menu myself. I know you are not vegan, so how did I do?"

I looked around at the spread of food on the table. It was the nicest thing anyone had ever done for me.

"You did all of this for me? I thought movie night meant pizza or something, but Marc this… this is so sweet. I'm really surprised."

"So, you will eat it?" he asked.

"I eat," I said. I'm sure I sounded defensive.

"I have been seeing you for what, about… five or six weeks, give or take a week? And in that time, I have only seen you eat an orange, possibly an apple and several smoothies, but I can't say that I have seen you eat. Oh, you might push a salad around a plate and pick at it, but I have never seen you eat. Don't you think that's strange?"

I was stunned by his comments. I didn't know how to react. Part of me was angry and wanted to lash out and say something like, "You don't have anything better to do but watch what I eat?"

Then, part of me wanted to tell him my whole life story about weight loss and my struggles, but I kept those emotions buried deep inside.

I decided to try laughing it off. "Whatever, Marc. You know I'm training. I don't always eat like that. I am on a strict diet so I can make weight for fight night."

"I have watched you starve yourself and workout like a crazy person. We are the same age and I'm not sure how you do it. You should be exhausted. What do you hope to accomplish?"

No one had ever asked me those questions before. I thought I had good reasons for fighting, but I couldn't think of a convincing answer when Marc asked me those questions. The truth is, I let my ego get the best of me, and now, I was getting into the ring with a girl half my age.

I stood there staring at Marc. He waited for me to answer and when I didn't, he spoke again.

"I have been a chef for a long time. I'm not a nutrition expert, but I do know that you can't lose weight by smoothies alone. What happens after the fight? Do you start eating regularly again? How much weight do you need to lose anyway? That's all you talk about; your weight and training."

"It's important to me," I said.

"Why? I love that you are health conscious, so many people aren't, but what are you doing isn't healthy, baby."

I wanted to hug him and tell him everything, but I didn't. I could hear the scale whispering, *"Are you gonna let some guy ruin all your progress? All this to get laid? Go ahead, let him see how you really eat. Eat that steak! Eat that giant fucking cookie too! Do it and then come see me. Do you think he really wants to see you naked? Do you want him to see you naked?"*

"Thanks for bringing the food. I really appreciate it. It was sweet, but you are right. I cannot eat any of this. I'm training to fight. I don't have to justify why I do what I do to you or anyone else. Who the hell are you to judge me?"

"I'm not judging you. I just don't think you are being smart about your training and what you eat."

"So, now I'm stupid?"

"I didn't call you stupid. I said you weren't being smart."

"Look, thanks for bringing the food, but I'm not really up for this after all."

"Oh, so now you want me to leave?"

"Marc, I don't need this shit right now. I am training and it is important to me. I really need you to back off. You might disagree with my methods, but they are effective."

"This is a short-term fix. A quick loss program with short term results."

"Are you done? You are just like everyone else, trying to stop me from being and doing what I want. I don't need this shit from you. I need to focus. Let me help you pack this stuff, so you can leave."

"Oh, so you're kicking me out?"

"Yes, Marc, this just isn't going to work out. I need to focus, and now, I see that you are a distraction."

"That's all I am to you? A distraction? I thought I was a little more than that."

"Well, you thought wrong." I snapped back. I felt like a crazy person inside. I was literally pushing this man away from me and I couldn't stop myself.

"Okay, well… okay," Marc said while packing up the food. He didn't say a word, he just carefully placed everything back into the bag. When everything was packed away, he picked up all four bags and walked to the front door. He turned and looked at me, "You know I like you for who you are. I'm not into head games and this feels like a head game. I'm too old for that kinda stuff. If you ever decide to stop playing games, call me." He walked out the door and did not look back.

The next day he did not call, nor the day after that. A week went by, no calls. I slowly realized that

Marc was gone, and I had pushed him away. My impulse was to eat, but that fucking scale was in my head.

"He had to go. He was a distraction. Bringing you all that food. He didn't know you were a tubby. It's good he is gone. More time to exercise. More time to dedicate to me. I'm always here for you. I understand fat girls. You are a fat girl. I get you."

I had convinced myself that Marc was a fluke and an anomaly, and truly I didn't deserve him anyway. I still wasn't worthy. I was constantly stepping on the scale, letting it guide my every move. Food became the enemy and I continued to spiral out of control.

I doubled down and threw myself into training. It was all I did. It was the only thing I had left. Andy was constantly pushing me harder and harder. He would mention my weight, as if calling me names was a motivator. He would say things like "come on biggie" or "move that fat ass". He never let me forget that I was the heaviest woman in the class.

I pushed myself until I had nothing left. I cannot describe to you the prejudice that one feels when they are ridiculed for being overweight. The world literally becomes your mirror and there is no escape. The more I listened to the scale; the more the answer to my problems was losing weight. I would be healthier, get Marc back, make Carl jealous with envy, my kids would be back, I'd do better at work, make new friends, and the list went on and on. Weight was somehow a factor in all of my issues.

****

The Friday night fight was one week away. I tried my hardest to forget about Marc. I had been training with Andy non-stop. I never mentioned what had happened at his party and I didn't speak to Paige either. I needed to focus. I had met Andy in the gym Monday night. The first thing he had me do was step on the scale.

"Holy shit, you weigh 195 pounds! You did it. How do you feel?"

Now, I could have told him the truth. The fact was I wasn't feeling well at all. I was thinner, but I felt tired and irritable. I was bloated and gassy most of the time from all those damn smoothies. I even tried adding a little fresh ginger to help with the stomach stuff, but it didn't seem to be working. I missed Marc. I missed Boonie. I missed my old life. So, what did I do in response to his question? I lied.

"I feel great. Ready to jump in the ring and kick some ass!" I tried to sound as upbeat as possible. Andy really didn't seem to notice or care.

"Great. We find out who you are fighting today. Excited?"

"Oh boy, I can't wait!" I lied again.

I stepped off the scale and went to wrap my hands. I sat on a bench, closed my eyes and took a few deep breaths. When I opened them, Felix was standing in front of me.

"Hey, you. You are really losing weight. Good for you. How do you feel? Ready for Friday?"

Why was everyone asking me questions? It wasn't in my nature to lie, but I was on a roll.

"I'm so ready!" I said, trying to sound enthusiastic.

"Great. Well, good luck. I have a class starting."

"Felix, does Sabrina still come to your class? I haven't seen her or spoken to her in a while."

"She comes from time to time, not as often as she used to. Anyway, gotta go. Later."

I hadn't seen Sabrina since the kids had tried their intervention. I tried to call a few times but got her voicemail. I never left a message as I was unsure of what to say.

I finished wrapping my hands and walked back over to Andy. He was talking with Paige and two other fighters. I stood and listened to him rant on about form, technique and power. He talked about being prepared both mentally and physically. After his little pep talk was over, we trained. The session lasted for about two hours. I was drained by the end of the night—I only had energy to unwrap my hands.

As I was packing my stuff, Andy walked over to me and sat down.

"You really pulled it off. You are fighting on Friday. You are fighting Paige. She requested to fight you. Said she could get in your head or something like that. She's a beast. How do you feel about fighting her? It's only three rounds."

"Absolutely," Again, with the lies. This was becoming something of a habit.

"Good. Now, we have to train hard for the rest of the week. What I don't need is excuses. I need you to be here." He stood and walked away.

Thanks for the pep talk coach, I thought to myself. I packed my stuff and walked to the car. As I started the drive home, panic crawled through me. I was fighting Paige. This woman was at least 25 years younger than me, stronger than me and yes, hungrier than me. I could literally feel the anxiety taking over my body. My breathing became rapid. I was afraid of fighting this woman.

All the doubt and fear I had suppressed over the past 7 months rushed out of me. I had to pull the car over and try to regain my composure. I put my head on the steering wheel and took in several deep breaths. After several minutes, I started to feel a little better.

I looked up and there it was staring back at me—*Burger, Burger, Burger.* I didn't even think twice, I put the car in drive and headed right to the drive-up window. I ordered a double bacon cheeseburger, the largest order of fries they had and a very large chocolate shake.

Once I got my food, I didn't even bother to drive home. I pulled into an empty parking spot and ate. I ate like I hadn't eaten in years. I don't think I even really chewed, just swallowed. It took less than ten minutes for me to devour the food. As soon as I finished the last bite, I burst into tears. I felt my stomach turn and my head hurt.

I was sabotaging myself. I didn't need fast food. I needed therapy. I was losing my fucking mind. I felt my stomach turn another flip. I opened the car door, leaned over and vomited everything I had just eaten. I sat back up and closed the door. I cried all the way home.

The first thing I did when I got in the house was make a beeline for the bathroom. I leaned over the toilet and vomited two more times. I really didn't feel well. I don't even know why I ate the food. I sat back up against the tub and cried. I had less than a week to fight Paige and I just devoured 1,200 calories in 20 minutes, and now I was puking my guts out—not a good look.

I leaned my head back, and then I heard it. That fucking scale!

"You need to weigh yourself. I'm waiting."

"FUCK!" I screamed.

I stood and stepped on the scale. I weigh 199 lbs. It was four pounds more than when Andy weighed me less than three hours ago. I felt myself beginning to shake, my palms were clammy, and I could feel my heart pounding in my chest. My breathing became labored and heavy. I could feel beads of sweat form on my forehead. The more air I took in, the harder it was to breath. I was having a panic attack; I was becoming unglued.

"So, I see someone stopped for a burger, fries and a chocolate shake. Nice going. I guess you really want to be fat forever. You still have the flab hanging off your arms, and you stop at the burger place? Once a fatty, always a fatty."

"SHUT UP!" I yelled. I picked up the scale and started to throw it across the room.

"I wouldn't throw me if I were you. You need me. You have less than a week to fight. Who is going to keep you honest? Who is going to tell you the truth? Who is going to tell you if you are worthy? I am. Right now, your weight is the most important thing in the world. Put me down!"

It was as if the scale had taken all the fight out of me. I caught a glimpse of myself in the mirror holding the scale above my head. I didn't recognize myself. I looked like a crazy person. I slowly put the scale down and left the bathroom.

I hadn't told anyone that I was having conversations with the bathroom scale. Honestly, I didn't know how to tell them. *Hey, things are good over here, just chattin' it up with my bathroom scale. Doesn't your scale talk to you?*

In all my years on this Earth, I was sure about one thing, I tend to sabotage myself. I almost will myself to fail at anything I try.

This this isn't always the case, but when it came to trying to lose weight, my wins didn't last long. I was always fearful of losing weight, and then, not being able to maintain the weight loss. That was the issue with most of the diets I had tried in the past. How long can you eat like a rabbit? Or eat special packaged food? Or drink your meals? When do you get to eat like a regular person again?

So, in the past, when I would make some progress while dieting, and nearing my weight goal, that hidden fear would rear its ugly head and I began to sabotage myself. I often wondered if others struggled as much as I did because it sounds crazy when you say it out loud.

****

The next few days, I didn't do much at all. I barely trained or ate, and I spent most of the time crying. I needed a friend and according to the scale, it was my only friend. I knew that I should have been training, but I didn't care. It's a strange feeling and very difficult to put into words. I knew that I would lose the fight, so what was the point of training? This was textbook for me: sabotage!

The chatter in my head went something like this; *how are you going to maintain 195 pounds? This won't last long? You should just stop now. What difference does it make? You're going to lose anyway. Don't you want a burger with everything? You pushed Marc away. You are really stupid. You are going to look so stupid in that boxing ring.*

I retreated. I called in sick and stayed home the next day. All day, I stayed in bed. I cried and slept most of the morning. By the afternoon, I ordered a pizza and by the end of the night, I had eaten the entire thing. I thought about calling Marc, but what would I say?

I avoided the scale the next morning. I wanted to call in sick again, but didn't. I spent the day hiding out in my office. Just my luck, it was someone's birthday and what did they have—you guessed it pizza. I helped myself to four slices and some dessert. I ate my pizza in the privacy of my office and inhaled every piece. I was in true sabotage mode. I just couldn't stop.

When I got home that evening, I thought running would be a good way to burn off the pizza. I went directly into my bedroom to change clothes. I should have been heading to the gym, but I didn't want to. My phone started to ring. It was Andy. This was the second day I was avoiding his calls or texts.

Once I was in my running clothes, I walked into the bathroom, forgetting just for a moment that my friend was there. The scale spoke, *"Running isn't going to make a difference? You will never be thin. You have tried your entire life. Why should this time be any different? You really want to sabotage yourself, step on me, let's see how much four slices of pizza are worth."*

I didn't reply. I simply left the bathroom and went running. I didn't get very far. I caught a cramp on my side, which sunk me to my knees. I managed to find a park bench and sat down. My breathing was rapid and erratic. It felt like I had never run before. I sat for a while, trying to get a rhythm to my breathing. I thought I might be having an anxiety attack, but managed to calm my breathing and slow down my heart rate. After a few minutes, I decided to walk back home.

As I was getting ready for work the next morning, the scale spoke to me again.

"You haven't stepped on me. You and I both know the numbers have increased, but just step on me and let's see where they stop. Are you over 200 pounds now? My guess is yes, but come on let's find out."

"Leave me the fuck alone!" I yelled—my voice rang throughout the bathroom.

"Leave you alone? We know that's not what you want. You need me. I tell you the truth about who you really are. I am your friend. I never lie. I am the one who tells you if you are worthy. I am the one who helped you get rid of some guy who was trying to fatten you up. I am the one who gets you."

"I don't need this shit today'" I said out loud. I left the bathroom and shut the door. Sometimes I would hear the scale when I wasn't in the bathroom, but it was the loudest when I was in there.

The day went by slowly. I stayed in my office, not really working. By the end of the workday, I had eaten a large grinder sandwich with fries, two of my boss's wife's cookies, a large mocha latte with all the fixings and a large bag of popcorn. So much for the fighter diet. I knew eventually I would need to go to gym and face Andy. I had avoided all communication with him for the past three days. His messages went from worry to anger. He started using all caps in his text messages.

That evening, I was in my kitchen when I heard a knock on the door. I had no desire to see anyone. I peeked out the window and saw Andy standing on the porch. He pounded on the door a few more times and left. Soon after, my cell phone starting ringing, it was Andy. Finally, after several calls and texts, I replied, *"I will be there Thursday to weigh in and train. Had a family issue."*

His next text was long. I could hear his voice as I read, *"Where have you been? I've been to your house; I've called and texted. What is going on? Don't make me look like a fucking asshole because you decided to quit three days before your fight. What is your problem?!*

I started to reply back but deleted the text. I knew he would have plenty to say tomorrow.

****

Thursday night, I went to the gym. As I entered, I saw Andy talking with Paige and two of the other girls. They were laughing and joking. When he spotted me, his demeanor quickly changed from happy to angry.

He quickly walked over to me demanding an explanation. I told him exactly what I had written in my text.

"Andy, I had a family issue. I'm sorry."

I knew I had been gaining weight, not drinking enough water, and overeating every chance I got. Andy huffed at me and told me to get on the scale. I weighed 205 pounds. This was probably mostly water, but it didn't matter because I had gained ten pounds.

"What is your problem? I haven't seen you since Monday. You fight tomorrow. You've missed every training session. Paige has been here. She's ready. What about you?"

"I'm ready," I said.

"Really? Because you look like shit."

"I haven't been sleeping all that well, that's all. I told you I had a family issue."

"Well tomorrow is fight day."

"I know. I've gotta go Andy."

"Go where, we need to run some drills, do a little sparring…" his voice trailed off. "What the fuck? What do you mean you're going? Look, I took a chance on your ass, and now you pull this shit?"

I had stopped listening to him and started packing my gear.

"Don't make me look like a fool tomorrow," he said. "I've invested in this fight too."

"Calm down Andy, it's not like it's a championship match or anything. It's an amateur fight."

"Amateur or not, a fight is a fight, and you look like shit. Who sabotages themselves a week before a fight?" He shot me a cold look.

"I guess those of us who were considered jokes," I grabbed my stuff. "I will be here tomorrow to fight Paige, then I'm done with you, her, and the fucking gym. So, after tomorrow you can fuck off."

"Well, you can fuck off now because I won't be in your corner. I train winners. You're a fuckin' loser!"

I started to reply but didn't bother. I just turned and walked out the door. Tomorrow was it for me. I started the car and put it into reverse when I heard Felix calling my name. I looked in my rear-view mirror and saw him running towards the car. I rolled down the driver side window.

"What is it Felix?" I was tired and annoyed. I didn't feel like a lecture on balance right now.

"I just wanted to see if you were okay. I heard you and Andy fighting."

"Oh yeah, I'm great. Fighting Paige tomorrow with no one in my corner. According to Andy, I'm a loser anyway, so put your money on Paige."

"I will stand in for Andy if you want."

I looked at Felix, a smile playing on his lips. I put the car into park and turned off the ignition.

"Really?"

"Yes, really, but on one condition."

"What's that?"

"That you stop this extreme training and dieting, and we focus on your overall well-being. Deal?" Felix held out his hand for me to shake.

I felt the tears rolling down my cheeks. I managed to nod in agreement and shake his hand.

"Now, go home and get some rest. If you can, take the day off, and sleep as long as you can. When you get up, I want you to take a walk, not a run, but a walk. I want you to think about all the good things in your life. I want you to feel gratitude. Can you do that?"

"Yes… yes I can." I wiped the tears from my face.

"Good. Here is my number. Call me around 2:00 pm tomorrow. I'll let you know where we can meet. It won't be here. We will come here together."

"Okay," I said, taking the small piece of paper from him. He smiled and backed away from the car. "Now, go home."

I shook my head, and started the car. This was the best I had felt all week.

Chapter 13

The following day, I followed Felix's instructions. I called my boss and told him I wasn't coming in and went back to sleep. I actually slept until 11:00 am. I got up, drank some water and coffee, and went for a walk.

I thought about everything that had happened in my life. I thought about my kids, Boonie, my job and my health. I thought about how I had lived through a very ugly divorce and how I had helped Frank and the others at the nursing home. I thought about how lucky I was to be alive and have friends and family who loved me, even though I had pushed them away. I was so deep in thought that I walked over five miles.

When I got back to the house, I showered. I didn't bother with the scale—what was the point? I called Felix. He told me to meet him at a small restaurant down the street from the gym at 4:00 p.m. I thought it was strange, but I didn't complain or protest. I tried calling my kids but got their voicemails. I called Boonie and got his voicemail too.

Around 3:30 pm, I left to meet Felix at the restaurant. I packed my gear and threw my bag in the trunk. I drove in silence, trying to control my growing anxiety and fear. I pulled into the parking lot and turned off the ignition. My stomach was turning flips. I thought I might get sick, but it quickly passed.

I walked into the restaurant and looked around. I thought I saw Felix sitting in a large booth with other people. As I started to walk in his direction, I could see Felix wasn't alone. Boonie, Sabrina, Marcel and Zaire sat at the table with him.

Part of me was happy to see them, but the other part of me, well, let's just say I put my game face on. I slowly walked up to the table. I stood there, not saying a word. I just looked at all of them and they were looking back at me. It was Felix who broke the staring contest.

"Hi. Sit down," he said, as he stood up and moved so I could sit.

I watched Boonie and the kids as their eyes stayed on me. I sat down and lay my hands on the table. I was nervous. I didn't know why. Hell, I had given birth to three of the five people at this table. You'd think they would be the nervous ones.

"So, did you follow my advice?" Felix asked. He was smiling, of course.

I nodded my head yes.

"Good, good. So, I gathered up everyone here today because I think you need some moral support in your corner. Fighting is just as much mental and physical. You have to be ready in both areas. I called Sabrina last night after we talked, and she filled me in on what has been going on."

I started to raise my hands in protest, but Felix put his hand up and stopped me.

"Now," he continued, "I think everyone at this table can agree that your transformation has been nothing short of spectacular. You have shown real dedication and commitment. That is something to be really proud of. But I think you lost sight of something along the way. Losing weight is important, but so is feeling good and being healthy. We are not here to talk you out of fighting, we are here to make sure that you still keep moving forward when the fight is over. Can everyone agree to that?"

Everyone nodded their heads in acknowledgment.

"So, with that, I think everyone has something to say before fight time," Felix said looking at Sabrina. She nodded her head and let out a heavy sigh.

"Mom, you know I love you. You know I… we only want the best for you. I was afraid when you said you were going to fight. I don't want to see you get hurt. I am proud of you. But I'm more afraid than anything else."

It was Marcel's time to speak next. Marcel was my stubborn child. He always spoke his mind and rarely backed down. He would say he got his stubbornness from me, which is probably why we bump heads.

"Mom, I think what you are doing is just plain stupid. It's dangerous. Why would you even put yourself in such a situation? For what? To prove some point? To who?" He stared at me with those dark brown eyes. I wanted to reach out and hug him because I knew what he was doing was out of love. But didn't I tell you he got his stubbornness from me?

"Look, Marcel. I know you are concerned, but I'm going to do this."

"But why?"

"It is something I must finish, Marcel. I need to prove something to me. Not you or anyone at this table, but to me. I know you all think I'm crazy, but I don't care. This is for me. My entire life I have done things for other people; you kids, your dad, my parents, his parents, my boss, and my friends. This time, is for me. Okay? So, you might disagree with what I am doing, but I need your support. Right or wrong, if you can't just be on my side to support me, then really, there is no reason for you to be here."

Marcel's eyes turned soft and somber. He looked somewhat defeated. He folded his arms and leaned back. He let out a sigh and shook his head.

"You could get seriously hurt," he said softly.

"I could, yes."

Zaire didn't say a word. He sat up and handed me a bag. I took it from his hands.

"What's this?"

"Open it."

I opened the bag and pulled out a black tank top. On the back of the shirt were the words "Bad Ass".

I smiled. "Thank you, Zaire."

"I'm with Marcel on getting hurt, but Mom, you could also kick ass."

I turned towards Boonie who had a small smile on his face—or was it a frown? I couldn't tell.

"You make me sick. I hate you, but I love you. Stupid. I am not taking care of your ass when you get out of the hospital. But I will say this. You look good. I'm real proud of your weight loss. You did that."

"I love you too," I said. He smiled at me, and just like that I knew things were good between me and Boonie.

We sat for a while longer until it was time to go. Although it was clear, no one was on board with me fighting, they were all going to be in my corner.

****

I drove to the gym alone. I needed time to get my mind right. I felt good that Boonie and the kids were at least going to be there. I was grateful that Felix was going to be there too. I pulled into the gym parking lot and parked in the furthest stall I could find. I turned off the ignition and sat in silence.

I'm not a religious person, but I do believe in something—you know, a higher power. At that moment, I was sitting in the car and I decided to talk to that higher power. I wouldn't call it a prayer, as it was more like a conversation.

"Hey, it's me. I know I don't reach out often but know that I do believe in something; the universe, source, God… whatever. Well, anyway, you know that I am about to fight, and I will admit, I'm a little scared. I mean, I'm older than the other girl getting in the ring. What I'm tryin' to say is that I don't move like I used to back in the day. I'm not asking to win, although that would be nice, I'm asking to just finish on my feet. I'm asking you to help me stand my ground. I'm asking you to help me to finish in one piece. I do believe in myself…well okay, I do have a little doubt, but that's okay right? It's okay to be nervous or afraid, right? Okay well, I'm going in now. Thank you for listening. Any help will be greatly appreciated."

I took a couple of deep breaths and got out of the car. I grabbed my bag, along with the tank top Zaire gave me earlier and went inside.

The energy in the gym was electric. I have never seen so many people packed into such a small space. They had set up folding chairs on all four sides of the ring. There were 8 rows on each side with ten chairs per row.

I felt the butterflies flutter in my stomach. I thought I might be sick, but the feeling quickly passed. One of the gym personnel walked up to me.

He handed me a sheet of paper and casually greeted me with a nod before walking away. The paper was the program for the fight. I quickly opened to see when I would be fighting. Because it was a heavyweight fight, it was listed as last on the program. I felt a little relieved, because I was last, but I was also nervous, because I was *last*.

I felt a hand on my shoulder, and I quickly spun around. I was happy to see Felix smiling back at me. He looked around the gym.

"It always looks so different here on fight night. The energy is different," he said while grabbing my bag. He motioned for me to follow him. He led me away from the ring and crowd, to the back into a small office. He waited until I was inside and shut the door.

"How you feeling?"

"Nervous."

"Oh, that's to be expected. I checked the program and we are last, which is good because it will give us time to warm up." He smiled and put the bag down on the floor. He sat down in the chair behind the desk and motioned for me to sit down.

"You got this. Don't worry."

"I'm worried. Maybe I made a mistake."

"Look, you've trained hard to be here. Take pride in that. Now, I thought you may want to change back here. So, get changed and meet me out front, okay?"

I nodded my head yes. He stood and walked out of the office.

As I started getting dressed, I could hear the announcer greeting everyone. I could hear the crowd jeer with enthusiasm. I listened intently as he rattled off each bout. I held my breath when I heard him announce each fight. There was no turning back now.

****

I stood in the middle of the office. My heart was pounding. Felix had just told me we were next. I was scared, but I took several deep breaths. Felix walked back into the office, smiling as usual.

"Hey, just remember it's only three minutes."

I looked at him and continued to breathe. He checked my hand wraps, helped me put on my gloves and grabbed the head gear.

"You ready?"

I nodded. I was as ready as I was ever going to be. He nodded and opened the door. I followed him out of the office, through the empty locker room and into the main room where the action would unfold. Having already seen seven fights, the crowd was pumped. I could hear cheering and chattering all around me. When we got to one of the corners, Felix stopped. He turned and looked into my eyes.

"You've done things I didn't think you could. You are here in this moment. No matter what happens, this is your moment. You've already won. Now, go and kick some fuckin' ass!"

He led me up to the ring and parted the ropes for me to slide through. I stood in the ring and looked around. The crowd roared when they introduced me. I was the challenger, of course.

I watched as Paige entered the ring, a cold look on her face. She looked directly at me.

"It's a mind game. She's trying to get into your head," Felix said, as he strapped on my headgear.

"It's working."

"Only if you let it," he replied.

We both watched as they introduced Paige. She waved to the crowd and stood on the ropes and held her hands up. I looked at Felix. He smiled and said, "You got this! This is what you trained for."

After a few moments, I met Paige in the middle of the ring. The referee rattled off the rules and told us to touch gloves. Paige stared at me and pushed her gloves into mine.

I walked back to my corner. I counted to ten and the bell rang.

Chapter 14

For those of you who don't know, an amateur kickboxing match is three rounds. Each round is three minutes. It doesn't sound like much, but you can take a lot of jabs and kicks in those minutes. Felix requested a minute rest after each round, and I was grateful that he did. My goal was to stay on my feet and not let Paige connect with her devastating overhand right. I had watched her hurt a few people with that punch.

You must focus. Everyone has the 'fight or flight' instinct. This is where you find yourself in a situation and you must either stand your ground and fight or run away (flight). This is a survival instinct. I believe most of us would probably run away from a scary situation, like someone trying to kick the shit out of you. In the ring you must mentally overcome the urge to run – the urge to take flight. Lastly, and most importantly, don't hold your breath.

Round one

As the bell rang, I looked back at Felix and he gave me a thumbs up. I quickly scanned the crowd and found my family, standing on their feet. They had signs that offered words of encouragement. There were the loudest people in the room.

I walked toward the center of the ring and put my hands up. I was greeted with a jab/hook combination and small kick to my right leg. I can't lie, that shit hurt like nothing I had ever felt before. I was a little stunned and instinctively started backing up. Before I knew it, she had me cornered. She showed no mercy as she pounded my head. I raised my hands and managed to push her back. I followed up with a right hook that, believe it or not, connected. Not a clean connection, but enough to let her know I wasn't beat yet. Paige followed with an intense overhand right that landed flush. I attempted to slow down the pace by pushing her into a corner. She came out with another overhand right, connecting flush on my left cheek. The pain radiated all the way through my body.

Thank God for referees—he split us up, but Paige came at me again and landed her third right. I ate the entire punch and dropped to the floor. Paige decided to throw one more strike while I was down. The crowd went crazy. I could hear Felix yelling that her move was illegal, and against the rules. The ref made Paige back off. My head was spinning and my ears were buzzing. I could hear the ref begin to count. I managed to stand at eight. I wasn't very steady on my feet, but the spinning had stopped. We spent the next thirty seconds trading shots on the inside. Paige caught me with an elbow and the bell rang.

I staggered back to my corner, looking for the stool before my legs gave out. All I remember was drinking water and Felix trying to give me some direction. Paige was out for blood and I had two rounds to go.

Round two

The bell rung and we touch gloves. I was surprised when the referee paused the fight to take a look at a cut above my left eye. After several moments, he gave the okay and we started fighting again. Paige landed another overhand right. She was trying to do more damage to my left eye. I could feel the blood dripping down my face, but I didn't feel any pain. I followed up by landing two rights of my own and managed to pull off the right roundhouse kick. I could hear Felix yelling for me to jab. I managed to back Paige off with my jabs and she came at me with a wild shot that missed. To keep her at distance, I used my kicks from the outside, but Paige is a good fighter and managed to get close enough to throw a few powerful body shots. I doubled over from the pain and was down again. I could hear Paige telling me to stay down. I managed to stand at the seventh count. The ref held my gloves and asked me if I was okay, I told him I was fine and we got back into it. As Paige came at me, I focused all my strength into an overhand right that connected flush on her jaw. She stumbled back and the bell rang. Round two was over.

I stumbled back to my corner. I could see Felix's mouth moving, but I couldn't hear him. My ears were humming. He put a gauze over my left eye and gave me water. After several seconds, the humming stopped and I could hear him.

"Are you okay? Do you want to continue?"

"Yes," I managed to say.

He nodded his head and gave me more water.

Round three

The announcer declared that this was the last round and asked the crowd to give both fighters a round of applause. Once the niceties were over, Paige approached with flailing punches. I managed to kick to the right side, which seemed to surprise Paige. I also managed a couple of nice combinations and followed up with an elbow, but I missed. I was getting tired, but was determined to finish this round on my feet. Paige came at me and landed four overhand rights that rocked me. I was practically on my ass. I could hear Felix saying, "You're almost there, jab, keep her off of you!" I jabbed twice and managed to back Paige off a little. She backed me into a corner and let her hands go. As I pushed her away, she butted my head. The referee called time and warned Paige. When the fight started, she was relentless, throwing punches and elbows. I managed to block most of them, but some of her punches penetrated my blocks and landed on my face. I pushed her and let go of my overhand right—it connected. Paige backed up and shook her head. She came at me throwing punches. All I could do was keep my hands up. When the bell rang, I fell to the floor. Felix jumped into the ring and helped me back to my corner.

I remember asking Felix, "Did I make it? Did I last all three rounds?"

He gave me a big hug and screamed, "Fuckin' right you made it! You did it!"

I fell into Felix's arms. My face was swollen and sore, and my body ached. I never felt better in all of my life. As we waited for the official announcement of the winner, I looked over at Andy. He was celebrating with Paige but managed to look my way. He gave me a nod. I'm not sure what that nod was supposed to mean. Maybe it was an acknowledgment that I showed up and finished—maybe it was an apology. I didn't know, but I did know that I had earned his respect, whether he admitted it or not. I earned the respect of everyone in that room, and it felt good. A sense of relief washed over me. I had trained for so long, and now, it was over in three three-minute rounds.

A few minutes later, the announcer motioned for Paige and I to stand in the center of the ring, where he announced Paige as the winner. He held up her hand and the crowd applauded. I watched her as she smiled and raised both hands in the air. Then, she turned to me and spoke, "You really surprised me out there. You ain't no joke, I'll give you that. Not too bad for an old lady. Much respect. I can admit when I am wrong, and I was wrong about you. You got heart."

"Thanks, Paige," I said.

Soon, the crowd began to thin out and the gym grew silent. I stood in the locker room staring at my face in the mirror. My face was swollen and bruised. Paige had literally beat the shit out of me, but I felt pretty good—sore but good. As I turned to leave, a little red-headed girl was standing in the doorway. It was the same girl I on my first day training with Felix at the gym.

"Hi," she said.

"Hi," I replied,

"You did really good lady."

"You think so?"

"I do. Why did you do it? I mean you are old, like my mom. She would never fight."

I smiled at her question. At least she said I was old like her mom and not her grandma.

"I had something to prove."

"To who?"

"To myself?"

"I don't get it."

"Well, when you get older, sometimes you do things that you normally wouldn't because you think it will make things better."

"How does fighting and getting beat up make things better?"

"Well, in hindsight… it doesn't. But I thought if I lost weight and did this fight, my life would be better. I thought if I did these things, my entire life would change, and I would wake up feeling loads better."

"Is it better?"

"No, not really."

"So, fighting didn't make things better?"

"I was fighting for the wrong reasons. Take you for example, why do you come to the gym?"

"Because my dad makes me. I was being bullied at school and he wanted me to learn how to defend myself. Kids would call me names like fatty and make fun of my red hair. I didn't like it at first, but I learned a whole lot and even made new friends. I have a friend at school, her name is Lacey. She gets bullied too. She is bigger than me and wears glasses. We are best friends. One day, one of the big kids called us fatties and took her glasses. They were all chanting "Fat Lacey has four eyes". I went right up to her and punched her in the face. I got Lacey's glasses back and told her to leave us alone.

"What happened after that?"

"I told Lacy that the only thing that matters is how she feels about herself. If she can learn how to like herself, then it won't matter if we're fat or skinny, wear glasses or don't. She's going to come and take the class too. Oh, and I did get in trouble for punching the girl, but it was worth it. My mom got really mad about it, but my dad didn't mind."

"It was nice of you to defend your friend."

"I thought so too. Me and Lacey may be called fat, but she is nice and funny. I like her, who cares if the other kids call us names. We are best friends. I don't think we are fat. Now the big kids leave us alone. That girl is scared of me, too."

"Oh, did you hurt her?"

"Not badly. It was a great black eye. She deserved it. Well, I just wanted to tell you I thought you did good, lady. My dad is waiting for me. See ya."

I watched as the little red-headed girl turned and left the gym. I thought about what she had said about Lacey and liking herself. *Kids are smart*, I thought. Smarter than me.

I grabbed my gear and walked out of the locker room. Boonie, the kids and Felix were all waiting for me. When I emerged from the locker room, they cheered. They all gave me hugs and high fives, which were painful, but felt good.

"Holy shit Mom, you were bad ass!" Zaire screamed. "I never knew you had it in you. You a beast!"

He hugged me. "Will you teach me the over-hand right move? That was the bomb when you rocked her shit!" Zaire's excitement was contagious. Marcel and Sabrina joined in his banter, and soon, they were all doing mock kickboxing moves.

"I'm going to take a class," said Marcel.

We all stopped and looked at him. Everyone was silent for a moment, then burst into laughter. As we walked toward the door, I looked at Felix and he smiled. He mouthed the words "good job".

Chapter 15

So you are probably wondering, *hey, what about the murder of your friend?* As I said in the beginning, it was a series of events that brought me to that moment. I have revealed most of what happened. I had lost weight, yes, but I wasn't the same person. My life did change, but it wasn't all good like I had imagined it would be. I thought if I lost weight, I would fall in love, be better at work, make new friends and life would be like some epic movie. I was wrong—so incredibly wrong.

I realized that I needed to change who I was on the inside, not the outside. No matter how hard I worked, I still felt like the fat woman in the mirror.

The day of the murder, as I've come to think of it, I had been in bed all day. I was still recovering from the beating I took from Paige, and although everyone seemed to be proud of me, I wasn't. I still felt the same. I thought some great transformation would happen. In hindsight, it was a really stupid thing to do. I could have really been hurt.

I actually let a bathroom scale dictate my life. Is that not crazy? Felix was right—I had no balance in my life. What good was it to lose weight if I wasn't healthy? If I didn't feel good.

I slowly got out of bed and walked into the bathroom. There it was… the scale. I hadn't stepped on it since the fight.

"Where have you been?" the scale asked. "Time to step on me and find out your worth. You know I never lie to you. We are friends. I'm your only friend. If you had listened to me, you could have beat Paige".

At that moment, I realized that I had become a slave to the scale and had measured my worth using it. The scale told me what to eat, when to eat, and how much to eat. It told me that if I were skinny, I would be worthy. It told me how to feel about myself and in turn, I lost myself. It was true, it never lied to me, but it didn't tell the truth either. I was more than that scale. I had almost lost my family, my best friend, my job, my life— all because of a bathroom scale.

I could feel myself filling up with rage. How could I have let things get so out of control? The scale told me it was my only true friend, and I had listened. I valued the scale's input so much that I went on a radical weight loss venture, for what? I left the room and grabbed the first thing I could find, an old baseball bat that I kept by the bedroom door.

It's done. Now, I'm sitting in the hallway breathing heavily. Nothing is left of my old friend. It was in pieces on the bathroom floor. So now you know how I came to this point—this overly dramatic gesture of killing what I considered a friend.

Like so many others, I put my worth in my weight. But I learned something. Something an eleven-year-old taught me—who cares what others think, you have to like yourself first. I am not my weight. I am much more than that.

****

Several days later, I went to the nursing home. They were in the process of getting him moved out when he became ill. I was told he could not be moved.

Frank had passed away two days earlier. They said he had become depressed; his daughter didn't visit and neither did I. I was told that he had left me something – I was given a small box and an envelope. I opened the envelope first and read:

My days are short. I miss seeing your face. At one time, you helped this old dog get his shit together. You did more than my own daughter ever did. But I know why you stayed away. It really doesn't matter now. I just want to leave you with this—we are all so busy looking at the outside of people, we rarely look inside and that is where the magic is… inside. I think you saw the inside of me, not the fat man everyone else saw. You are special, even if you don't believe it.

The doctor says I have a heart blockage. They are trying different drugs they want me to try, but I am ready to move on from this life and this world. I was hoping to see you before it was my time, but I'm already gone if you are reading this. I left you a small present. Remember to be who you are. Don't let others' opinions shape you. You are beautiful inside. Thank you for showing an old, fat man love.

Frank.

I opened the box and inside was a picture of a very young Frank and his wife. He looked so different—he was thin and smiling. They were holding hands. Under the picture was a small ring. I'm guessing it was his wife's wedding ring. He also said he kept one possession of hers, but never mentioned what it was. I slowly put the ring on my pinkie finger and felt a tear roll down my face.

Later that day, I met Boonie for lunch at our spot. It was like old times. He told me about his many dates, his daddy-daughter time with Ivy, and his new job. I missed him so much. It was so great to have my friend back.

"Girl, when I saw you take that punch from that beast, I just knew it was lights out, honey! But you kept getting up. But I'm proud of you. I love you. You were never fat to me. I love you forever honey—fat, thin, doesn't matter. I always liked what was inside."

"Fat Lacey," I said.

"Who is fat Lacey? Did I miss something?"

"No, you didn't miss anything."

I was glad we had started talking again. I missed my friend. I decided to tell him about Marc and the last time I saw him. Boonie was thrilled at the idea of a new love in my life, but very displeased at how I handled the situation.

"Girl, what is the matter with you? How long did this love affair last?"

"About six weeks… give or take," I said.

"Six weeks of love and you let him walk out the door?"

"I was a crazy person then, Boonie. I even stopped talking to you and my kids! I pushed everyone away and for what?" I stopped and looked down, "He was so sweet, Boonie. He was kind, considerate, funny, and quirky. We had so much in common."

"Then, why are you here talking to me."

"Really? This isn't some great Hollywood romantic movie where I head off to find him and all is right with world, Boonie. This is real life. My life. He said when I stop playing head games to call him."

"Well?"

"Truth?"

"Yes, honey, the truth."

I sighed and said, "The truth is that I am afraid to call him. I couldn't bare the rejection. Boonie, what if he tells me to fuck off or is seeing someone else?"

"Call him and stop talking like a crazy person!" Boonie said. "You will know what to say. You always do. You really sell yourself short. Are you the same bitch I saw kick some ass in a boxing match not too long ago?"

"You mean the bitch who got her ass kicked," I laughed.

"You did it. You got in that ring and stood toe-to-toe with a beast. I wouldn't have done that shit for no one. Call the man. And by the way, you look really good. I mean it. You look good. Healthy… happy… It's a good look on you."

"Thank you, love. I think I am finally getting comfortable in my own skin."

****

Several weeks later, I got a call from Felix. He was opening a new gym and asked me to teach a class. It had been his dream to open his own gym, and he was finally in a position where he could make a move. It wasn't as big as the boxing gym, but it had a welcoming energy that the boxing gym didn't have. He didn't have a boxing ring, but he did offer kickboxing and other classes, free weights, machines, group training room, showers, and a big sauna.

Felix and I kept in touch since fight night. He had become a friend. We had lunch a few times and I really got to know him. I was happy to hear his dream of opening his own gym was becoming a reality, and even more surprised when he asked me to teach a class. I told him I had no experience, but I was willing to try.

Felix asked me to teach three days during the week and every Saturday. The class would last one hour, and I could teach whatever I wanted. I decided to teach a low impact kickboxing class. I choreographed the moves and picked all the music. My class was made up of older women who were just looking for a good workout. My debut class was small. I forced my kids and Boonie to attend and I had three students. It was a little scary, but after a while, it started to become fun. My class got bigger, and soon I had students of all ages, shapes, and sizes.

It was great to see people eager to work out and have fun. People were so willing to share their stories and listen to others. Many found that they had similar experiences or felt the same way. I watched as the class grew larger and I even had my 'regulars' who came several times a week.

It made me realize that so many of us had struggled to lose weight and fix our body image issues. Having someone who can relate to your struggle can ease the pain and offer hope.

The idea of helping one another spread like wildfire. The class has started a Facebook page and shared their successes, recipes, and fitness tips. I watched as women motivated and pushed one another, gave encouragement, and made everyone feel at ease. I wasn't even the skinniest or the most fit person in the room, but I didn't care. I felt good inside. I wanted to help others feel that way and let them know they are not alone or crazy.

I am learning to have balance in my life and figure out that being healthy is not necessarily being thin but feeling good inside and out. Since I have stopped training, I have gained about ten pounds and love every blessed pound.

When I stopped training, it was important for me to be comfortable in my own skin. It was also important that I maintain my weight and focus on nutrition. I learned this over a lifetime. There is no short cut to losing weight—no magic pill or diet plan.

'Losing weight' isn't the best term for a long-term solution. It has a negative connotation in my mind. I decided to make a 'lifestyle change'. It was less impeding and was easier for my mind to accept. I still eat my boss's wife's cookies but have learned to limit myself. For the first time in a long time, I feel pretty good about my future. I know that being over fifty isn't old and I can do whatever I set my mind to.

My advice to you is to love who you are. Don't compare yourself to anyone—you are unique. Learn to love yourself. You are not alone in this journey. And most importantly, if you find your bathroom scale talking to you, don't listen; the numbers on the scale don't measure your worth—you do.

****

If you are wondering what happened with Marc, I can share this with you. Today, as I sit here writing, I received some mail. There was nothing unusual, and I started to toss it in a drawer, when a small postcard fell to the floor. On the front was a picture of a new restaurant opening downtown. I bent down and picked up the card. I turned it over and there was a handwritten note from Marc.

Hi. I hope you are well. It has been a while since we last spoke. I miss you. I have been busy and, as you can see, opening a new restaurant. The grand opening is next week. I hope you will attend. Marc.

I had been too afraid to pick up the phone to call or text him and now, in my hands, is an invite to his restaurant grand opening. I was truly happy for him.

I am not sure what will happen. But I have learned that life is what you make of it. I get up and walk into the bedroom. I need to find the perfect outfit for Marc's opening.

As I push passed the clothes, I come across my old flower mumu. I pulled it out of closest and laid in on the bed. I dawned on me that I was finally the after person in the picture. I bawled the mumu put and threw in it the corner. I smiled because I knew I would ever be the before person again. I was the after person.

I must admit, it felt good.

The end.